DUKE OF CHRISTMAS

PREQUEL TO THE SEARCHING HEARTS SERIES

ELLIE ST. CLAIR

Facebook: Ellie St. Clair

Cover by AJF Designs

Do you love historical romance? Receive access to a free ebook, as well as exclusive content such as giveaways, contests, freebies and advance notice of pre-orders through my mailing list!

Sign up here!

Also By Ellie St. Clair

Standalone
Unmasking a Duke
Christmastide with His Countess
Seduced Under the Mistletoe Multi-Author Box Set
(featuring The Duke of Christmas)

Happily Ever After
The Duke She Wished For
Someday Her Duke Will Come
Once Upon a Duke's Dream
He's a Duke, But I Love Him
Loved by the Viscount
Because the Earl Loved Me

Searching Hearts
Quest of Honor
Clue of Affection

Hearts of Trust
Hope of Romance
Promise of Redemption

The Unconventional Ladies
Lady of Mystery

1

1784

"Whatever do you mean, Jane, he has a taste for depravity?"

Marie Colemore stared at her friend as horror began to churn in her belly, along with another emotion she couldn't quite identify, but it seemed something akin to excitement. According to Jane, her closest friend, Marie's intended fiancé, a man who was not only one of the most powerful dukes in England but one of the richest, had tendencies of which one should never discuss. Surely that was not something to be particularly excited about. But at least, finally, she was learning something about him — something more than could be found in Debrett's. And perhaps, she had found a way out. The man hadn't shown a glimmer of interest in her and, in fact, had outright ignored her. Now she knew why.

"I only mean..." Jane looked around her furtively, to ensure that no prying ears could overhear their conversation. "My brother — you know he has always had a particular fondness for you, Marie — mentioned to me that perhaps you should be aware of the duke's particular ... proclivities."

Marie took her friend by the wrist and pulled her from the crowded ballroom, looking one way and another before finally choosing an open door. Once they were through the entrance, the door closed behind them, Marie released Jane and made her way over to the carved giltwood mint green settee, taking the seat closest to the roaring fire in the hearth.

"Tell me more," she demanded, and Jane, her oldest friend, as blonde and tall as Marie was dark and small, took a seat across from her, primly sitting on the edge of the matching Chippendale side chair.

"My brother went to school with the duke, you know — to Eton. They have been friends since childhood, and the duke drew acquaintances to him easily, with his charm and his title. It is not often a current duke finds himself at school, but then, that is what his father had wanted."

Marie knew the Duke of Ware's father had died when he was quite young, and he had practically grown up with the title. Unlike some, however, who frittered away the wealth and responsibility received at a young age, he had always seemed rather respectable — responsible, even, keeping his name out of the scandal sheets.

"Anyway," Jane continued. "Already having the responsibility that came along with the title, the duke decided for himself that he couldn't go about causing scandal with young ladies as many of the other young men did. Oh, he had a good time to be sure, but he didn't want to make his activities as public as some others did. He already had a great deal within business investments and that sort of thing."

"I understand and know all that," said Marie, impatient for Jane to get to the heart of the matter. She had made it a priority to search for information on the movements of the man she would one day marry, despite his persistent denial of her. "Carry on."

"Right," Jane said with a nod, and she twisted her hands in her lap. "You know, of course, that the duke is an attractive man…"

Marie nodded. Of course she knew that. She had met him on occasion, but that had been years prior. She hadn't spoken to him in ages — since his father had died. He had been a very young man, while she was still a child. It seemed that in his will, the former Duke of Ware had expressed an interest in his son being married to the daughter of his oldest friend, a friend he knew would raise his children with the utmost propriety. It was true that Marie's parents, the Marquess and Marchioness of St. James, had ensured in recent years that their children learned to be acceptable members of society, but they had allowed Marie a great deal of freedom in her youth. When her mother tried to harness all of that energy to raise her daughter to become a respectable bride, it was, perhaps, slightly too late. For by that time, Marie had ideas of her own, and her mother now despaired, believing it was her own fault the duke so blatantly ignored her daughter.

"Well, it seems," Jane said in a whisper now, though the room was empty save the two of them, "he began frequenting a brothel, as did many other young men, of course. But then the *madame* took an interest in him, and he in her. And then—"

"While I am enjoying your tale, Lady Jane, I must say that you are getting some details wrong."

Jane let out a yelp of fright, while Marie whirled around

3

in her seat to the direction of the voice, with its deep, rich tone that sent chills down her spine. She searched in the shadows to see who was speaking but saw no one — until the figure stepped out into the light.

Her heart stopped. It couldn't be.

But yes, of course, with the way her luck continually seemed to turn, it was.

"Lady Marie," he said, sauntering over to the settee where she sat frozen, despite the heat thrown by the fire beside her. Her eyes locked on his as he bent over her hand, picking up her fingers and bringing his lips to the back of it. "How lovely to see you again. You look beautiful, as always."

"Th-thank you, your grace," she said, finally pulling her eyes from his to look at Jane, who sat on her chair with her mouth wide open.

"Tell me, Lady Jane," he said, straightening, though he didn't let go of Marie's hand. "How fares your brother? It has been some time since I have seen my dear ... *friend*. You will have to give him my regards. Now, would you give me a moment alone with my betrothed?"

Jane squeaked out something unintelligible but looked at Marie, who gave her a nod, telling her she would be fine. It was improper, true, but what was the worst that could happen at this point?

∾

So THIS WAS HIS BRIDE.

Lionel took his time perusing her from head to toe, and she knew it, too — she squirmed in discomfort but didn't take her eyes from his, and he was impressed that she didn't shy away from him. Though not his type — no innocent lady was — she had the look of a little vixen, her dark, jet black hair piled high on her head, her shockingly crystal blue eyes staring back at him from a face that would make a sculptor's fingers itch.

He leaned down toward her, running the pad of his thumb over the soft skin of her cheek. She jumped a bit but didn't lean back.

"Was what Jane said true?" she asked boldly, her eyes searching his, and he raised his eyebrows at her.

"Do you want to know?"

"Of course I do," she answered, straightening her shoulders.

"Very well, then," he said, smiling at her as he sat in the chair Jane had vacated, the wood creaking from his weight. He certainly was a big man, his shoulders broad and his chest wide. "Some of it is true, yes. I have certain tendencies that I enjoy, but nothing out of the ordinary. Besides, there is nothing for you to be frightened of. I should not expect you to fulfill those needs — unless you want to, that is."

She finally broke her gaze away from him, looking at the floor, the only sign of her reaction to him the twitching of her fingers.

"You will fill those needs elsewhere, then, is that the case?" she asked, meeting his stare again, her chin set resolutely.

"I suppose that is what I had thought to do, yes," he said with a shrug. "I find that seems to work well for most married couples."

Marie sat still for a moment before leaning forward in her chair.

"I don't think I altogether like that idea," she said matter-of-factly, and he raised an eyebrow, though inside he was smiling at the thought that she was already becoming possessive of him. In fact, he rather liked it.

He leaned forward, picking up a long strand of her dark hair from where it framed her face, curling it around his finger.

"Don't do that," she said, wrinkling her nose as she swatted his hand away.

"Do what, my sweet?" he asked, bringing his face closer to hers.

"Touch me," she said, though she didn't move away. "And I am not your sweet."

"No?" he asked softly, his lips now but a breath away from hers. "Was I misinformed? Are you not Lady Marie Colemore, daughter of the Marquess of St. James, who my father was so insistent on me marrying?"

"Yes, but—"

"Then, you are my sweet."

"But—"

He silenced her protestations as he leaned in and took her lips with his. She was to be his wife — why not have a taste? He could sense her shock as she stilled for a moment, but she didn't sit back, didn't push him away. Lionel didn't force anything further on her for the moment, but simply allowed her to enjoy the sensation of what might very well be her first kiss, before he began moving his lips over hers, at first softly, but slowly growing in force. He leaned over her now before gently pulling her up toward him, wrapping his arms around her, and twining the fingers of one hand into her hair.

When the tip of his tongue teased the seal of her lips, she opened to him with a bit of a moan, sinking into him, and he held her even closer. He didn't know how long he stood there kissing her, tasting her, but eventually, desperation for her overcame all else as he wanted her in more ways than would be proper to act upon with his betrothed in a drawing room at the home of one of the *ton*'s leading peers.

He eased back from her, leaving a kiss on her forehead, before placing her back on the settee and returning to his chair as he watched her with a smile on his face. Her shock wore off quickly, soon to be replaced by a fierce attack on him.

"Why did you do that?" she demanded, to which he laughed.

"Because I wanted to. You liked it, didn't you, sweet?"

"I'm not your sweet."

"You are now, love."

"Or your love — *your grace*."

"My, aren't we formal for a couple that is going to become so intimate so soon, are we not, Marie? Call me by my given name, will you?"

"And that is?"

He was a bit surprised she didn't know, given that they had been pledged to be married for some time now, despite the fact they had hardly spoken.

"Lionel."

"Your name is Lionel?"

"It is," he said, wanting to laugh at the incredulous expression on her face. "Do you not approve?"

"It's simply ... not what I expected," she said, shrugging one delicate shoulder. "It wouldn't be my first choice, no, but I suppose it will have to do."

He did laugh now, wondering how this woman, the daughter of a marquess, spoke so openly of what she thought, unlike the typical lady of her class. She would keep him on his toes, to be sure — when the time came to wed, that is. "Well, you will have to take it up with my mother, I suppose, as she was the one who chose it."

"You wouldn't tell her!" Marie exclaimed, turning wide eyes on him, and he chucked her chin softly.

"No, I'm just teasing you," he said. "Of course I wouldn't tell her. It will be difficult enough to wrest control of the household away from her once we marry. I shouldn't want to make it worse."

"What do you mean?" she asked, her eyes narrowing now. "You believe it will be difficult for me to get along with your mother?"

"Most likely," he said nonchalantly. "She has been running my house and my life since I was fifteen. When I fully took on my duties as a duke, I left her to continue managing the household as she wished."

"I see," said Marie, biting her lip. "I have to say, your gr — Lionel, I am beginning to think this situation is not altogether ideal."

"No?"

"No," she said with additional resolution, standing and beginning to pace, her lips turned in a frown. "In fact, I think this is all a huge mistake. I will speak to my father tonight and tell him to call this entire thing off. I do not want to be married to a man who has already decided he will take other women to bed, meanwhile leaving me in a house with a woman who only wishes ill of me!"

"Very well," he said, crossing one leg over the other, enjoying watching her stride back and forth over the carpet with such force, he thought she would wear right through it. "I shall find another wife, then. It shouldn't be overly difficult. When the will was read, it seemed you would do well enough because of your lineage and your dowry, and I figured it didn't make much of a difference, so why not? I am thirty now, so I suppose at some time I should actually consider marriage to a respectable lady who will provide me with an heir. But if you're opposed to the idea, I will speak to the solicitor tomorrow and arrange everything to be called off."

She stopped pacing and stared at him, her mouth agape.

"That's it? You really don't care?"

"I do not."

"You ... you ingrate!"

And with that, she whirled around on her heel and stormed out of the room, slamming the door in her wake.

2

Lionel chuckled to himself as he re-entered the ballroom and scanned the crowd for a sign of the little minx, soon catching sight of her in the corner with her friend, the sister of the dastardly Lord Downe. He knew the man had put ideas into his sister's head to pass along to her friend. Clearly, the man was trying to get closer to Lady Marie himself, and Lionel wasn't about to allow to happen. Not anymore.

Lionel could admit, however, that he had lied to her.

He'd told her he didn't care which young woman he married as long as she would do well by the family and provide him with an heir. But as the words spilled forth, he was shocked when he realized that he no longer felt the same as he had but an hour before.

Now that he had met Marie Colemore, daughter of the Marquess of St. James, he had a different outlook altogether.

Despite her protestations, he *would* make her his bride. She tempted him, that he couldn't deny. The dark strands of her hair which curled around the edges of her heart-shaped face, the red bow of her mouth that was so delicious under his — he groaned with his desperation to truly make her his. With a woman like that, there was only one way, and he figured if he had to take a wife, why not one that was as delectable as this woman?

Lady Jameson, a widow who had entertained him a time or two before, caught his eye across the room, but her low décolletage and her sultry smile did nothing for him tonight. No, there was only one woman who was stirring him, and he would do all he could to make her his.

A smile curled at the edges of his lips as he sought out the Marquess of St. James, drawing him over to stand against the wall.

"Lord St. James, I must speak with you regarding the betrothal between me and your daughter," he said, and a worried look crossed the man's face, his eyes flitting back and forth across the room from beneath his powdered wig.

"I hope she has done nothing to offend, your grace," he said, his head lowered. "She can be a sprightly thing, 'tis true, but no woman is better suited to be your bride than she, that I can promise you. Her mother and I have trained her well—"

"She has done nothing of the sort," Lionel responded, considering how entirely suitable she had actually proven herself to be. "In fact, I would like to officially announce the betrothal, to move up the date of our wedding to just past Christmastide once all return to London."

"So soon?" the Marquess' bushy eyebrows rose in surprise. "Are you sure? Will all be prepared? Is that enough time? I—"

"I find myself in need of a duchess sooner rather than later," Lionel said smoothly, though with a hint of censure in his tone. "Should Lady Marie not suffice, then I'm sure another young lady would be more than willing."

"Oh, no, very well, your grace, very well. Whatever you wish."

As close as the Marquess of St. James had been with his father, Lionel enjoyed keeping the man on his toes. He always was a bit of a pompous sort, and Lionel enjoyed toying with him.

"I'm glad to hear of it," he said, shaking his hand. "I will call upon you tomorrow, for a proper introduction with Lady Marie."

"As it happens your grace..." The marquess looked slightly uncomfortable, and Lionel raised his eyebrows.

"We are having a house party in the country for Christmastide and are leaving tomorrow," he continued. "We had not thought to invite you as ... well, you had not previously shown interest in attending any of our events. However, if this has changed, of course, we would be more than pleased to have you join us."

He looked at Lionel with some trepidation.

"I should always like to be invited to your parties from here on," he said smoothly. "I will see you on the morrow."

As Lionel walked away, he could see the marquess scurry over to his wife to share the news, and he enjoyed a laugh at the man's expense.

MARIE TWISTED her fingers in her lap as she waited the next day late in the afternoon in the drawing room of her family's country home near Reading. They were but a couple of hours from London, though it felt as though they were days away, so quiet it currently was. Though not for much longer. Their guests were to arrive any moment, although there was one in particular that was causing her more consternation than the rest, one who had promised to arrive before all others.

She was so deep in her musings that when the knock came on the door, she jumped and nearly fell from her seat, catching herself before she slid down the sofa's velvet covering.

"The Duke of Ware," the butler intoned in his staid, dry voice with which he introduced everyone and everything. She figured a beggar off the street or King George himself could be at the door, and Shepherd would announce them all the same.

She stood, curtseying as the duke entered, her mother and father following behind him. Her mother looked as though she had been gifted chocolate pudding, her father sending Marie a look of warning not do or say anything untoward.

"Your grace," she said in greeting. "How lovely to see you again."

"Again?" her father said. "I had thought this was an introduction."

"I have had the pleasure of seeing Lady Marie at various events," the duke said, and Marie narrowed her eyes at him. Yes, he had seen her, but last night was the first time he had ever truly spoken more than a word to her, so intent he had always been on ignoring her, trying to escape his commitment.

"Yes, that is true," she said, and as he walked over to select a black brocade overstuffed chair, he winked at her with a wicked grin. Her eyes widened that he would be so bold in front of her parents, but they either had not seen anything or chose to ignore him. For what were they going to say to a man like the Duke of Ware?

Her father always despaired of the fact that the son was

nothing like the former duke. He enjoyed life far too much, the Marquess would rant, shirking his responsibility of marriage to her. Well, apparently not anymore.

"We are so pleased to have you among us over Christmastide," the marchioness said, fawning so heavily over the duke that Marie had to keep from rolling her eyes. Yes, how wonderful that he finally decided to join them, acting as though they had been remiss for not inviting him, when in fact he had turned down multiple requests to join them in the past. "It will be the perfect opportunity for us to become better acquainted before the season truly begins."

"Yes," added Marie, with a purposeful bite to her tone. "How lovely you have chosen to grace us with your presence."

"Marie!" her mother said sharply, and Marie smiled prettily at them all in turn in order to take the edge off of her words.

"Might I have a moment alone to speak with Lady Marie?" the duke asked, and her father looked somewhat put out.

"I am not sure that would be altogether proper—"

"A moment will be fine, Hartford," her mother said, placing a hand on his arm with a look of reproach in her eye. "We will be just outside the door."

Her father gave each of them a look of warning before leading his wife from the room.

Marie glared at the duke.

"I had thought I made myself very clear last night that you were free to find yourself a new duchess."

"Yes, well, I decided that you, in fact, Lady Marie, will become my duchess."

"Why the sudden interest?" she asked, standing and slowly advancing on him. "All this time, you never bothered to even speak with me, to dance with me, let alone even mention a word of our supposed betrothal. I had no idea if I should be entertaining the interest of other gentlemen, or be sitting and waiting for you to deem it time for us to come together. I do *not* enjoy being toyed with, your grace."

"Oh no?" he said, rising himself, his body strong and taut, and he walked toward her, meeting her in the room's center. He came but inches from her, and she had to force herself still to keep from backing away.

She refused to give in to his man who tried using his size to intimidate her. She was not one of the usual sort of simpering misses, and she would be sure he understood that.

"No," she said with force, poking a finger into his chest. He reached down and caught it, burning her fingertips. He lifted her finger and brought it to his lips, and she could do nothing but stare as he kissed its tip. Damn. She should have worn gloves this afternoon.

"I think," he said, and she cursed her fickle heart for noticing the dimple in the left side of his cheek when he smiled, "that you would enjoy being played with, Lady Marie."

She wrenched her hand back from him.

"We are talking *marriage*, your grace. About tying our lives together for the rest of our days," she hissed. "Do you not take *anything* seriously?"

He grinned lazily at her, which only served to further anger her. "Not really," he said. "We don't know how many those days will number. Why not enjoy them as best we can? I'm sure we can find some sort of enjoyment together. And if we tire of one another, well," he shrugged, "We can find others to help us pass the time."

She gasped and retreated a step. She knew it was the

way of many marriages, but this was the second time in two meetings he had spoken of such, and she could not believe he would continue to be so crass.

"I am very aware that my father will likely force me to go through with this marriage," she said, hearing the bite in her tone. "But this week, *your grace*, shall be a very good indication of what is to come."

"Will it?" he asked, his eyes hooded, and she stepped back a bit more, as much from her own response to him as the way he looked at her as though she were a tall glass of brandy set in front of a man with an unquenchable thirst.

"Yes," she said, her nose in the air as she mustered all the authority she could with him so close to her. "Here is what we will do. You will court me, as though I am a woman you just met, one that you feel you could be interested in. And I will respond as though you were a *gentleman* who has just begun to show me regard. Perhaps we will find ourselves drawn to one another. Or perhaps, we will find that we are being led toward a life of misery."

"I have made my choice," he said, advancing toward her. For each step he took forward, she took another back until she jumped when her back came flush with the wall behind her, and she took a breath as he dipped his head toward her. "We *will* be married, Lady Marie. So it is time you quit trying to tell me what to do and accept what is to come."

She wanted to be furious with him, to rage at him that he could not speak to her so. But all thought left her as he filled the space between them and his lips came down on hers.

L ord, but she talked far too much. That mouth of hers moved constantly, and he didn't enjoy the orders that came from it. He was going to tell her to be quiet, to leave him be for a moment, but the easiest way to keep her from speaking any longer was simply to otherwise occupy her lips. He had been longing to kiss her again anyway, so it seemed the ideal time to do so.

She tasted as good as she had the first time, although now, as angry as she was, she relaxed into him much sooner, having previously experienced his kiss before. Somehow she was soft and sweet, yet passionate and fiery. He groaned as she fueled his growing desperation, which was unlike anything he had ever felt before.

He slipped his tongue through her lips, and as it touched hers, she jerked back violently away from him as though he had burned her.

"Stop it!" she hissed, though a hand unconsciously came to her lips. "You cannot distract me with your kisses. I'm not like one of the loosely moral women you spend most of your time with. I — I must be going. I will see you at dinner."

And with that, she was gone, out the door so quickly it slammed forcefully behind her. Lionel poured himself a glass of brandy from the sideboard, filling it near to the top. It was the Christmastide season, after all, and a time to celebrate. He took his drink and sank into a leather wing armchair as he brought it to his nose, inhaling the rich sweet scent. He normally avoided house parties, for they bored the life out of him. This one, however, was already proving to be very interesting indeed.

WITH NO FOREWARNING of the attendees, Lionel had no idea who he would be greeting when he walked into the drawing room before the first night's dinner. His eyes immediately settled on Marie, who turned her back and pretended not to see him. She was speaking with a very pretty blonde woman, whom he thought he recalled was the wife of Marie's brother, the Viscount of Lovell. A fine gentleman. They had run in similar social circles until the man had been married a couple of years prior. Now a husband and father, he was no longer interested in the gambling hells Lionel enjoyed, nor even the odd visit to White's.

Lionel recognized many of the usual crowd, about a dozen people in all, in addition to the family. Some were lords and ladies looking for a match of their own, others were couples who were more interested in a fun holiday season than one alone with family.

There was Lady Jane, whom he recognized, of course, as Lady Marie's friend. And her dastardly brother, Lord Harry Totteringham, Earl of Downe. God, he hated the man. They had been rivals since their days at Eton, and apparently, they would remain that way.

He narrowed his eyes as Downe approached Lady Marie, but he said not a word, determined not to show any sort of emotion, no matter how annoyed he was at the man's ludicrous attempts to draw closer to Marie. Instead, Lionel sauntered into the room, pleased to find an old acquaintance, Lord Whitby, in attendance.

"Ware! Good to see you, chap," Whitby said as Lionel entered the drawing room, attracting many curious stares from the assembled guests. He knew he was something of an enigma to many, a duke who was rarely seen at *ton* events, but he preferred to find himself in establishments where it didn't matter quite as much that he was a duke. "Whatever are you doing here? I had no idea you were to be among the guests."

"Neither did I — nor our hosts, as it happens, until yesterday," he replied, clapping Whitby on the shoulder. "Now, what do you say, shall we find ourselves a brandy?"

"It seems as though you've started without me," Whitby said with a twinkle in his green eyes, not a strand out of his blond hair out of place. "Have you seen the Lady Jane this evening? She's a beauty, is she not?"

"I suppose she is," said Lionel with a shrug, though in truth he had only noticed that she was in the room and not anything further. "I am here for one woman, and one woman only, Whitby — my betrothed, the Lady Marie."

Whitby looked at him in shock. "You're going through with it, then? I have to say I was rather surprised to see you here, given that you've been avoiding the woman and her family for years now."

"I have decided its past time," he said with a casual shrug.

"Would that happen to be because of Lord Downe and his not-so-hidden designs on the woman?"

"Not in the least," he replied with a snort of derision. "I have no concerns regarding the Earl of Downe."

"No?" Whitby asked, an eyebrow cocked. "Then you are not worried that the man is escorting your future wife out of the drawing room and into dinner?"

"What?" Lionel whirled around to see it was as Whitby described, and he turned to follow them without another word to his friend, though he thought he heard him chuckle as he stalked away.

~

OF ALL THE NERVE.

Marie had brazenly flirted with Lord Downe just paces away from the Duke of Ware for several minutes now, and he hadn't even bothered to take a second glance at her. Why she was trying to get under his skin, she didn't know. The man infuriated her, and she wanted nothing more to do with him. In fact, she told herself, she would prefer that he leave, denounce their betrothal, and never return.

But she couldn't deny the impossible allurement she had to him, and she wanted to know — no, she *needed* to know — if she was more than just a game to him, if he really did care at all that she was his betrothed. If he wanted to marry her so badly, then he better well show it. And so, she tried to coax out the one emotion that shouldn't be any issue — jealousy. But he had stood there, sipping his damn brandy and talking to Lord Whitby as though she wasn't even in the room.

She took Lord Downe's arm when dinner was called, though she somewhat bristled at his nearness, as she could sense the leer he sent down at her. Marie loved Jane and had been the best of friends with her since they were girls, but

Jane's brother always made her feel somewhat wary. His brown hair was curled around the top of his head, his facial hair cut into the smallest of triangles on his chin, his thin lips above it always curled into a sneer when he looked at her. His eyes were dark and narrowed, and Marie shivered a little as he placed his hand over hers, drawing her in closer.

She kept her head facing forward, refusing to look back to see if the duke had even noticed. They entered the dining room, where the staff had begun to include hints of the season. Bits of evergreen, ivy, and holly — the house's namesake — lined the middle of the table, and the fireplace crackled merrily in the hearth while the candles in their sconces high on the walls cast shadows over the mahogany sideboard and table. Was that a ball of mistletoe hung from the ceiling? Marie wouldn't put it past her mother to try to force more than one alliance during this party. Then she could always boast of how her parties brought the young people together.

Marie, however, made certain to give the mistletoe a wide berth. Lord Downe pulled out Marie's chair, placing a hand at her back as he pushed the chair in, and Marie finally raised her eyes, stilling when they were caught by the duke across the table.

His lips curled into a grin as he took her in, his dark blue eyes boring into hers before they began to travel down her body and then back up again. She shivered again, but this time not with the chill of Lord Downe's touch, but with a thrill of anticipation.

Stop, Marie. You are angry with him.

He leaned back his chair away from the table, one leg crossed over the other as though he were relaxing in his own library and not sitting at a dinner table with fifteen other people.

He spoke for a moment with Jane beside him, his eyes crinkling at the corners when he smiled, and Marie tried to ignore the way her stomach began to churn when they glimmered. She was not jealous of Jane for simply talking to the man; the very notion was absurd.

Marie watched as his gaze turned to her before flitting around the table with disinterest, finally settling not on her, but on Lord Downe to her right. Was she imagining things, or did his eyes narrow with disdain?

"Lord Downe," he said, rolling the bottom of his drink around on the table, keeping the liquid from sloshing out of the glass. "Tell me, how fares Mrs. Monk?"

Marie jumped when Lord Downe spit out his drink, choking as he did so, and the duke grinned.

"Who is Mrs. Monk?" she asked, looking from one of them to the other.

"She is an ... acquaintance ... of Lord Downe's," the duke said, placing his glass on the table.

"And how fares Lady Featherington? Or Lady Dauncer? Or any of the women at the Handy Horse Club?" Lord Downe asked.

Marie's heart began to beat wildly when she realized of what they were speaking, and she straightened her spine as she let out a loud sniff of disapproval to tell them precisely what she thought of their conversation.

"I wouldn't know," said the duke, ignoring her, "for I have not seen any of the women you speak of in some time now. Anyway, now that we have discussed our acquaintances, perhaps we should move on to discuss something more ... proper. Would that suit, Lady Marie?"

Perhaps he had noticed her after all. She nodded, though she kept her nose high to show him her displeasure that he had even begun the conversation.

"The weather has been lovely this winter, has it not?" he asked, mocking her, and she didn't know whether to laugh or snarl. She decided to do neither and instead, played along.

"Yes, your grace," she responded. "I so look forward to skating tomorrow."

"Oh, skating are we?"

"We are."

"I recall we skated quite frequently in our youth, did we not, Ware?" asked Lord Downe.

"We did," said the duke, his blue eyes glinting. "I rather enjoyed besting you on more than one occasion."

"I seem to remember things differently."

"For the love of God," said Marie finally, her frustration getting the best of her. "When the two of you have finished, please notify me and I will rejoin your conversation. Until then," she picked up her fork and paid attention to the plate in front of her, "I will enjoy my meal and pretend neither of you is here."

4

Lionel suffered through the gentlemen's after-dinner conversation. He was surprised to find he had much in common with the Marquess of Burrton, despite the fact the man clearly held himself in fairly high esteem. He kept waxing on about Lionel's luck in securing a "diamond of the first water," but besides their mutual admiration for women of their acquaintance, they also shared a love for horseflesh, and became engaged in an animated discussion of what to expect at Tattersalls come the spring.

He had to admit, however, that he was most looking forward to rejoining the ladies, and he couldn't keep the smile off his face when they entered the room and he saw Lady Marie attempting not to look at him.

But he knew. Intense attraction simmered between them, and before this house party was over, he would convince her of how much better it would be if they were to both act upon it.

After politely welcoming the other women in the room,

he slowly sauntered over to Marie, who was with her friend, the Lady Jane.

"Might I have a word?" he asked, and at her curt nod, Jane left them, and Lionel assumed her place in the red velvet chair. They were near the pianoforte, upon which one of the young women in attendance was playing "Adeste Fideles," though rather poorly. At least the music would drown out their conversation, leaving them in some privacy.

"I have not yet had the opportunity to tell you just how becoming you look tonight," he said, his voice low and smooth, complimenting her as he knew ladies always appreciated.

"Oh?" she said, an eyebrow raised and her lips drawn together. "Tell me, your grace, do you really think you can walk over here, flatter me with your contrived words, and then hope to return to my good graces?"

Well, most ladies appreciated his compliments. He was stunned at the bite to her tone, not used to being rejected so heartily. And she wasn't finished. "You have proven, your grace, that you care not one bit about my actions, so why do you have such a mind to marry me? Why, I could have kissed Lord Downe soundly on the mouth right in front of you, and you would have cared nothing at all."

"Oh, Marie," he said, hearing the thickness in his voice as he leaned into her. "How very wrong you are. For had Lord Downe come another inch closer to you, you would have known my dismay very well indeed."

"Is that so?" she said with a sniff, her eyes turning to focus on something in the distance. "I would have thought otherwise."

"Why do you care so much, if, as you say, you have no wish to marry me?" he asked, his grin widening.

She shrugged and attempted to feign nonchalance, but he wasn't fooled.

"It is not that it matters to me, I just thought that if you were to marry a woman, you might be upset to find another man trying to steal her from you."

"Am I at risk of losing my betrothed to Lord Downe?" He lifted an eyebrow, and she raised her nose higher in the air, if it was at all possible.

"Perhaps."

"Then you are a fool."

She bristled and he tried not to laugh.

"You — you—" Apparently she could not find a word to properly describe him. "You *scoundrel!*"

Finally, he gave in and laughed, heartily enough to draw a few stares.

"I've been called much worse," he said.

"I wish you had never come here," she hissed, and he deduced that she was likely just as angry at herself as at him, for he could tell that beneath the anger simmering on the surface, she was as drawn to him as he to her.

"I say, Marie," he said, feigning extreme hurt, "that is not an entirely polite thing to say to a guest — particularly your future husband."

Marie stomped her foot and lifted her finger, apparently ready to tell him exactly what she thought, but then her gaze shifted behind him. He gathered they were likely attracting more than a casual look from the other guests, something that would never do for Marie. She took a deep breath, gathering herself once more.

"I believe I am simply exhausted," she said primly. "Good night, your grace."

He turned in his chair in order to watch her go. She bid goodnight to the other guests, never once looking back at him. But Lionel didn't mind. Instead, a smile began to spread over his face as he thought of the days to come. This certainly wouldn't be their last conversation. Far from it, in fact.

LIONEL RUBBED his hands together as he looked out over the ice in front of them. While he would never admit to such, he was actually looking forward to the day. He had always been a rather proficient skater, and he was never one to hide his talents.

He risked a glance over at the fiery hellion who had pointedly ignored him since last night. He didn't know what her issue was. He was being perfectly charming and had done nothing but tease her as he would any other woman. His worst offense was being honest with her, but he didn't see the point in beginning a marriage with a lie. He supposed he would have to win her over, though *how* he wasn't entirely sure. None of his usual methods seemed to work on her.

After lacing his skates, he slid out onto the frozen pond, enjoying the sound of the blade crisply cutting the ice. He cut from one side to the other, becoming used to the sensation again. It had been some time since he had skated, and as he looped around the pond's edge, the freedom of his youth came rushing back with the wind in his face. He came to a stop when he returned to join those who had decided to partake in today's activity, and his attention couldn't help but be drawn to Marie. Her dark curls had been pulled back and tied away from her face with red ribbon. Her cheeks were rosy with the cold and the exertion, and her crystal blue eyes sparkled with mirth in the day's bright sun.

Lady Jane was at her elbow, and Jane's brother, damn the man, was standing close at attention. Lionel smiled, however, when he remembered Downe from their youth. The man was as athletic as a newborn foal.

"I say," called Marie's brother, Lord Lovell, who was heir to these lands that stretched far into the horizon, "What do you all say about a race? We can begin at one end of the pond and go right across to the other."

The party heartily agreed, and before long, they were all lined up, lords and ladies alike. Lady Lovell, who had accompanied them but cried off from participating as she said she had no skating ability, agreed to count them down, and soon they were off, heading across the pond in a chorus of shouts, giggles, and calls.

The pond was near to the size of a lake, and Lionel quickly found himself in the lead. When he looked back to see if there were any threats, he was shocked to see that Lady Marie, while a ways back, was leading the rest of the pack, despite the heaviness of her skirts which she held up from the ice.

Someone near the middle of the group suddenly slipped on the bumpy ice, and skaters went down with a shout, though plenty of laughter arose from the group. Marie became his sole challenger, with but a few gentlemen chasing her down.

He saw himself nearing the lake's end, and he slowed, ready to stop and declare his victory. As he waited for the others, however, he realized that Marie wasn't slowing down — not at all. He noted the determination in her eyes as she neared, and he held out his arms toward her.

"Lady Marie!" he called. "Slow down, you are going to—"

He couldn't finish his sentence as all the breath fled his body when he went flying back into the snowbank behind him, bowled over by the runaway horse that was Marie. When he collected his wits and opened his eyes, it was to find her lying overtop of him, her face filled with exhilaration, as he felt the rapid rise and fall of her chest after her brilliant skate.

"I won!" she said, raising an arm in triumph, and despite the fact that he was thoroughly enjoying her body stretched out atop of him, he moved her down to his lap as he sat up fully.

"I say, now!" he replied in mock anger. "I finished moments ahead of you. Anyone can attest to the fact."

"Yes," she said with a smug grin on her face, perched atop him like a queen who had just won her throne. "But you stopped."

"I was at the end of the ice!"

"Nearly. You were a foot short."

"I have never been part of a race that ended in a snowbank."

"Well, you are now." When her eyes flashed, their fire sending more heat — were it possible — straight through his entire body, despite the fact he was lying in snow.

For a moment, Lionel had forgotten they were not alone — until another voice cut in.

"Ah — perhaps we can call it a tie," said Lord Lovell dryly, who reached out a hand to help his sister to her feet, giving Lionel a warning look. "Good race, everyone. Why do we not enjoy ourselves for a bit before returning to the house?"

Marie began to skate away, but Lionel was like a child following a tray of pastries fresh from the oven, as he couldn't help but chase her down, pleased to find that Lady

Jane was nearly as bad a skater as her brother and therefore could not keep up with her friend.

"You enjoy competition," he remarked when she glanced sideways at him.

Her gaze flicked his way briefly. "I do."

"And you are fiercely determined," he added.

Another fleeting glance. "I am."

"And rather athletic, I should say."

"Do you find my womanly attributes lacking, your grace?" Her eyes lingered a bit longer.

"Quite the contrary, Marie," he said, unable to keep his voice even, hearing it deepen as his mind went places much warmer than this frozen winter day. "I believe all of those traits to be more than admirable. They are rather ... alluring, actually."

This time she didn't glance over at him, and he could tell he had disconcerted her. She had been prepared for another barb, not a compliment. But, true to form, she couldn't keep herself from speaking for long.

"I am unsure whether I should be complimented or insulted, your grace," she said as they rounded the corner, and he noted how perfectly in time their feet were.

"Oh, definitely complimented," he said. "There is much more where that came from, Marie. I look forward to exploring and admiring your many other attributes."

And with that, he skated off, a wide grin on his face.

5

Marie dressed with care that evening, donning her favorite crimson gown. Gold lace edged the sides of it, revealing her matching gold petticoat beneath, while a floral design in green covered the front panel. The red hue was perfect for her coloring, she knew, and the square neck framed her bosom perfectly. Marie had given her maid careful instructions to ensure her dark curls cascaded just so from the top of her head, while she applied enough rouge to her cheeks to look as though they were naturally flushed.

She would like to deny that it was all for *him*, but, of course, it was. He infuriated her to no end, and yet she wanted him to be attracted to her, to see her and no other. How ridiculous was that?

As she descended the curved marble staircase of Hollyvale Manor, a warmth blazed through her chest, as large as the fire around the Yule log. It was Christmas Eve, and while they had been skating, choosing the Yule log, and preparing themselves for dinner, the staff had draped the house in greenery. Holly and boughs from evergreens had been draped over the staircase banister. Hanging at intervals from the ceiling — how in heaven's name they ascended that high she wasn't sure — were balls and boughs of mistletoe, ivy, and rosemary. The fresh fragrance of the greenery filled the entire house, bringing a sense of pleasure to Marie's heart. She had always loved this time of year, a time when family and friends gathered, and all seemed right with the world.

She was so preoccupied with gazing around that it took a moment until she sensed a presence below her on the stairs. Her eyes widened as she spotted Lionel awaiting her. Oh, but he was handsome, the devil. His black coat, embroidered with golden flowers, nearly matched her own dress, though he couldn't have known her ensemble ahead of time. His dress was fairly simple, a fawn shirt atop his black breeches and white socks, but she didn't think she had ever seen a better looking gentleman in her life.

His wore no wig, nor powder or curls in his chestnut hair, but rather allowed the loose waves to fall naturally from his forehead into the tie at the back. She longed to run her hand over it, to see if it was as silky as it looked, but for a moment she could hardly even move, nor think, nor speak. It was only his eyes that pulled her down the remaining stairs, one footfall after the other, until she was standing in front of him on the last step, their eyes level. Her heart seemed to be beating in an uneven pattern, and she fought to catch her breath.

"Good evening," he said, his voice low and sultry.

"Good evening," she managed, biting her lip when she heard just how breathless her words were, but he either didn't notice or didn't care. He held out an arm to her and began to lead her to the drawing room. Suddenly she didn't want to go in there, where the rest of the world awaited them. She wanted to remain with him, alone, where no one else would intrude.

She stopped, and he turned to look down at her, concern etched on his face.

"Is everything all right?"

"Your grace, I—"

"Lionel."

A tiny thrill coursed through her at the thought of using his given name.

"L-Lionel?"

"Yes. It's my name, and I'd like you to use it."

"All right then — Lionel," she said, feeling as though a wall had come down between them, and suddenly they were standing on the same side of it, ready to take on whatever was to come — together. Except she forgot what it was she was going to say, as all she could focus on was his face in front of her, his arm beneath her fingers. "It's Christmas Eve," she finally managed.

"It is," he responded, a small grin now lighting his features. "'Tis the season of mistletoe."

"Of — what?"

"Mistletoe. And you, my Marie, are standing beneath some."

She gave him a look of disbelief but then tilted her head back and found that, sure enough, a lush bundle of green was hanging overhead, its white berries gleaming in the light of the chandelier. Her breath stilled.

He had kissed her before, true, but somehow that had been different. That was before she came to learn just how wonderful he could be when he truly wished to be so. Before, he had kissed her without warning. Now she was choosing this as much as he. She raised her face to him, offering her lips, and when she felt nothing, she opened her eyes, feeling rather silly at her expectation. She gasped in shock to find he was but a breath away, and when he saw her look up at him, he grinned, teasing her, and then finally caught her lips with his. It was not the passionate kiss of before, not one that was backed by any aggression, but instead, it spoke of something else, something that told her perhaps this man who seemed so indifferent to everything and everyone around him actually cared about something — could it be her?

The kiss was over so quickly that when he stepped back, she found herself leaning into him, longing for more, but when he moved his head down toward hers, it was to bring his lips to her ear instead.

"Come to me tonight."

"What?" she gasped, pulling back from him to look into his face.

He released her, returning her hand to his arm, and said nothing further as he looked over her shoulder and nodded to Marie's parents as they entered the room.

"Good evening," said the Marchioness of St. James. "How lovely the pair of you look together. Do they not make a fetching couple, Lord St. James?"

"Why yes, they do," Marie's father said, though his brows drew together and he directed a look of disapproval at how close they were standing.

His obvious censure only emboldened Marie. This was what they wanted, was it not? She drew ever closer to Lionel — she had to admit it was lovely to think of him by his given name — and the four of them made their way into the drawing room.

~

DINNER WAS TORTUOUS.

Marie sat across from him, and despite the luxurious courses that appeared one after the other in front of him, all Lionel could focus on was the delectable bosom that seemed to be right in his line of sight.

After the soup dish was whisked away, he caught Marie looking at him with a raised eyebrow and then a frown, and he smiled in apology. Instead of her...attributes, he must focus on her face — equally as beautiful — or he wouldn't make it through dinner.

Every time he looked at the greenery decorating the table, the only thing he could think of was the mistletoe he had so conveniently found himself beneath with Marie earlier in the evening. He wanted to kiss her again, but he wasn't sure that would be enough. The woman had bewitched him, and he wasn't entirely sure what to do about it.

The worst of it all was that it wasn't just her body that called to him. No, the woman had a clever mind and a wicked tongue, and he felt he could sit back and listen to her speak all day.

"I, for one, do not agree with you Lord Burrton," she was now saying, and Lionel was completely oblivious to the topic of which they spoke, so focused had he been on his own musings. "Why should women not have the right to work if they so choose? Or to be, at the very least, involved in discussions regarding a political nature? For the decisions of parliament affect each and every one of us, not just men."

"Marie!" her mother admonished from down the table, and Marie shrugged, clearly unconcerned about her mother's distress. When Lionel flicked his eyes to the marchioness, she was clearly motioning toward him, and he wanted to laugh. For if the woman was concerned her daughter was scaring him away with her words, she was quite mistaken. No, Marie's intelligence was more attractive than even she could know. She knew what she wanted, and she spoke her mind. It was sexy as hell. As long as, that was, she didn't try to control *him*. Of that, she would have to be careful.

Dinner was agonizingly long, but it finally came to a close, as everything did, he supposed, and when the marchioness called for a dance, he wasn't sure whether he wanted to celebrate or bemoan her declaration. It was an excuse to be close to Marie, but he wasn't sure he could stand it.

When they entered the ballroom, his eye was drawn to the gilded edges framing paintings of tiny cherubs, which circled in the same gold frames bordering the room. He and Marie came together without words in mutual under-standing as Lady Lovell sat at the pianoforte and began to play the first notes of "The Christians Awake." This family certainly loved the Christmastide season.

As the idea entered his thoughts, suddenly Lionel forgot that he typically dreaded Christmas. Since his sister Bess had married, he usually spent this time of year in a gambling hell, not wanting to be around families who gath-ered, inviting him only so they could say they had a duke in attendance. His own home remained unadorned over Christmastide. Bess, with her vivacious spirit, had always been the one to bring Christmas into the house, and when she had married and moved across the country, he had decided he no longer cared. But now that he was here, with the energy flowing around him, he cared more than he wanted to admit. It wasn't Christmas he despaired of. It was the reminder that he was all alone, and no drinking buddy or buxom barmaid was going to fill that void.

But, perhaps, there was someone who could. Marie came into his arms, her tiny frame fitting him perfectly. They moved together in unison, and he held her close, wanting to spend the final evening hours with only her.

"You move gracefully for a large man," she said, and a laugh rumbled in his chest at her words.

"I am not sure if I should be complimented or not," he responded.

"Oh, you should," she said, tilting her head to the side, her curls spilling over her cheek. "I wouldn't have thought a man like you would care to dance."

"I enjoy it with the right partner."

Her cheeks reddened, deeper than the rouge she must have applied — was it for him? He laughed again. "You, Marie, are an excellent dancer, as I am sure you well know."

"Yes, well, my mother ensured that I excel in the skills expected of a duchess. I would not want society to think less of me."

"Do you really care so much of what others think of you?"

She dipped her head. "No. Yes. I — I'm not sure, your gr- Lionel. There is a part of me that would love nothing more than to let it all go, and I really wish I could just be myself all the time. But when one has been raised in such a way, to always be concerned, it is difficult to forget, is it not?"

Thinking on his own background and the fact that he had never had a childhood so much as an education in becoming a duke, he could understand some of what she was saying. Except that he rebelled against everything that had been pushed upon him, and wanted nothing more than the freedom to do as he pleased. But then again, there wasn't anyone around to tell him otherwise.

The dance ended too soon, and Lionel was more annoyed than anything to find Lord Downe at his elbow.

"May I have this dance, Lady Marie?" the man asked, ignoring the glower Lionel trained on him.

"You may, Lord Downe," she said, but Lionel's chest swelled when her eyes remained upon his.

"Tonight," he whispered, before bowing and stepping away to find himself a much-needed drink.

6

Marie could hardly make it through to the evening's end. Her stomach churned as she considered Lionel's request. Given the way she tingled all over and her middle fluttered when the notion played itself in her mind, her body wanted to go to him, that much was certain. But if she went ... there would be no going back. He was her betrothed, to be sure, but they were not married yet. What did she truly know about him?

When the other guests began to retire, she slowly walked to her own chamber, as she debated what it was she intended to do.

"Marie!" She halted. Was that her name being called? She turned her head one way and then the other, but saw only the sculpture against the wall on one side and a painting on the other. She had never known there to be ghosts in Hollyvale before. Maybe they decided she needed some help.

She heard her name again, and finally determined it was the statue speaking to her. Well, something behind the statue, that was. She peered around it and nearly screamed in fright when Lionel stepped out from behind. His hand came to cover her mouth for a moment until her heart resumed its regular pattern, and then he released her, a finger held against his lips.

"Come," he whispered. She should say no, should turn away and continue onto her room, but it seemed she could not help but to follow him, wherever he might lead her.

He maneuvered around her home with unexpected ease in the dark, and before long, Marie found herself in the library. Lionel lit a candle, casting a dim light through the room. It was her father's room, really, and the dark chestnut furniture with the navy walls as a backdrop somehow created an even deeper feeling, one that well suited this clandestine meeting.

"What are we doing here?" she whispered, though she strongly suspected why. She also very well knew that she needn't whisper, for they were the only ones present.

"You seem nervous," he said, his voice coming out in a low rumble as he stepped closer toward her, and she could finally make out his features in the dim light. "You needn't be. I do not plan on doing anything untoward in your father's library."

"But I thought..."

"That I asked you to meet me in order for me to take your innocence?" He raised an eyebrow.

"Well ... yes, as a matter of fact." Marie was proud of herself for keeping her voice steady, despite the turmoil she felt churning inside her. She wanted to tell him just how contrary he was, but the greater issue was that he made her contradict *herself*. Never in her life had she thought she would be willing to give herself to a man before she married, even if that man was to be her husband. Yet, here she was, upset that Lionel didn't want to take her virtue.

And then there was him. He was so aloof, so unconcerned about anything around him, but this was simply how he was. Why did it bother her so?

Because she wanted him to care. About her.

"Why did you ask to meet me, then?"

"Because," he said, taking a seat in her father's favorite chair, the walnut bergere. He slouched back, crossing one leg over the other. "I wanted a chance to spend time with you alone, to get to know you better. We are certainly attracted to one another, that much is clear. If we are to spend the rest of our lives together, should we not get to know each other a little better?"

She sat across from him on the edge of a framed elbow chair, keeping her shoulders back and her posture straight. "What would you like to know?"

This wasn't the way of things. Typical courting was not sharing one's inner thoughts with a man. Rather, it was casual teasing, coquettish smiles, harmless flirting. She would have to be careful.

"What do you like to do with your time?"

"My time?"

"Yes, your time. Do you enjoy painting? Embroidering? What else is it that ladies such as yourself do to entertain themselves?"

"Oh. Well, I have always been close to my brother, until he married that is. I suppose when I was younger I spent much of my time chasing after him outdoors, spending time on our Hollyvale's grounds."

"And now?"

"Once I was old enough, my mother ensured that my time was spent preparing myself in all of the ways of a lady. For my come out, for ... marriage."

"Marriage to me."

She looked at him closely, trying to see beyond his words, behind his hooded gaze as he stared at her from across the room. Was that possessiveness she heard in his tone or was she simply imagining things?

"Why must you prepare when we are to marry anyway?" he asked, so nonchalant that his question irked her. "All of this pomp, the gossip, the dresses, the riches that fathers spend — what is the point of it all?"

"We were born into this life — these are the circumstances we have been given," she responded slowly. "I did not choose to be born the daughter of a marquess any more than a poor woman in St. Giles chose to be born into her family. I understand how fortunate I am to be provided this life, Lionel, I do. But I will not apologize for caring about how I look, or the latest fashions, or what is currently of interest to the *ton*. How do you care nothing about it at all?"

"I care in my own way."

"Do you really? And what of you, then, your grace, what do you do with your time?" she asked, though her heart beat faster in anticipation of his answer, nervous about what he would say, whether Jane's words were true.

He looked away from her for a moment before returning his steady gaze to her face.

"I told you to call me Lionel."

"Lionel, then. You never answered my question."

"I like to enjoy myself," he said simply, and she raised an eyebrow.

"And who looks after your estate?"

"Primarily my mother."

"Ah, yes, your mother. I have had the ... good fortune ... to meet her on occasion."

Each time Marie had been in the same room as the woman, she had kept her distance. For Lionel's mother, the duchess, did not hide the fact that no woman would be good enough for her son, and she had made it clear that she found Marie lacking. She was disparaging to all of them — to Marie, to her mother, even to her father. Marie could tell the woman wished her husband's will had never been found.

"I believe she may be joining us later this week."

"What?"

"Your mother suggested that I invite her," he said with a shrug. "So I did."

Good heavens, she was the last person in all of England Marie wanted in her home, but it was not as though she could tell the duke that. Her mother cared simply *too* much about appearances. Her ire raised now, she lost any hesitation dictated by manners.

"So tell me, Lionel, how *do* you enjoy yourself? Gambling? Women? Drinking?"

"I suppose you have the way of it."

"Is that all you do for entertainment?" Truly, Marie was jealous more than anything.

"Do I detect envy in your tone?"

She looked at him sharply, realizing he was laughing at her.

"I just wonder at something, Lionel," she said, her hand on her knee, her back stiff straight. "You have been all but betrothed to me for years, and yet you have never deigned to call on me, never attended any party with me, never asked me to dance, never even *spoke* to me. Why, I believe when you saw me coming you ran the other way. Why this sudden interest?"

"Because," he responded, looking up at her. "I met you."

HE WASN'T sure what had come over him. For she had been right — he had asked her to meet him tonight in order to act on his urge to show her all the ways of physical love between a man and woman. Somehow, however, it didn't seem quite right — not yet. She was to be his wife. She was innocent. Before now, he had made certain to avoid entanglements with the uninitiated. It seemed, however, that everything had changed.

When she spoke, he listened. He longed to know more about her, to hear her every thought and opinion. It was mystifying. What was it about this woman? Her ideals were unlike any he had ever heard another woman confess to, let alone openly speak of. He had met women who cared nothing for the *ton* or their way of life, true. But Marie was an odd blend of a bluestocking and a woman who cared for her reputation.

She was jealous, he knew, and she had the right of it. He had ignored her for far too long out of his fear of committing to a woman, of changing his entire life. It didn't seem so terrible anymore.

She looked slightly uncomfortable at his admission.

"You say this," she said, tilting her head to the side, "but you have spoken of finding other women if the marriage should not go well, of ours being simply a marriage in name, like so many others we know. While I understand it is quite common, I do not like that idea. I do not like to share, Lionel. But you, well, you don't seem to care."

"Perhaps you care too much," he said, studying her, her beautiful pixie face now in turmoil. "Perhaps you have to let go of your preconceived notions, the fact that you need to have everything so tightly under your control, in order to find your zest for life."

"You assume too much, Lionel," she said, raising an

eyebrow. "You think I do not enjoy life, but the truth is, I enjoy my life very much. Is it too much to ask for a husband who might care for me, who would treat me as a wife should be treated? I will admit that I am attracted to you. But yet I wonder if you could be that person, the husband I need."

"You are wrong to think I could not be, that I do not care," he said. "It may not always be obvious, Marie, but I care very, very much."

He had told himself he would just speak with her, would simply get to know her better. But she looked so proper, so perfect sitting across from him in the most uncomfortable chair he had ever seen in his life, that the only way he could prove how true he was to his word was to show her.

He crossed the few feet between them in moments, taking her hands and lifting her to her feet. This kiss was not gentle, but rather, he took her in his arms with a possessiveness he didn't know he was capable of, showing her with the way his lips ravaged hers that he cared, more than she could know.

She raised her hands, smooth and cool upon his whiskered cheeks. He embraced her tightly, an arm around her back as he drew her close against him, feeling every soft, luscious curve of her body. His hand came up between them, as he was unable to keep from feeling the mound of one of her small yet exquisite breasts. He had never thought a breast could fit so perfectly in his hand.

Marie cried out when his thumb and finger teased her nipple, and he lifted her tiny body and placed her down on the sofa. The skirts of her crimson dress were so voluminous that he had trouble finding where they opened, but when he was actually determined about something, he was a difficult man to stop.

Once he found her smooth, satiny leg through layers of

45

red and gold, however, he knew his course, sliding his hand up her muscled calf and over the inside of her thigh.

She jumped slightly at his touch, breaking her lips away from him to whisper, "That tickles."

Ah, so his little minx was ticklish. He grinned, saving that information for later.

She apparently tickled no more, however, when his hand went higher, finding a place reserved only for him. He felt how ready she was for him, before he continued on to find her nub, and he began to stroke her lovingly. Her gasp in his ear was galvanizing, and he captured her lips again to keep her from crying out, drinking in her moans as he took her to her release. Finally, when he knew she was complete, he eased back from her, caressing her cheek with the knuckle of his finger. She looked up at him, her face replete in satisfaction.

"Never think I don't care about anything," he ground out before sweeping one last kiss on her lips, re-arranging her skirts, and then striding from the room before he did anything more that he shouldn't.

7

"So, tell me," Jane said, her eyes inquisitive, "what has occurred between you and the duke?"

"What are you talking about?"

Jane raised a brow as she eyed Marie with an inquisitive grin. "You have been staring at him all morning, and he at you. Clearly, something has changed."

"It is Christmas, and I am to marry the man," Marie replied as impassively as she could manage. "Should I not have some feeling toward him? I am simply imagining what *next* Christmas shall be like, not in my own home but his. Perhaps I shall be the hostess of my own party."

"You, a duchess," said Jane dreamily.

Marie looked sharply at her. "Never tell me you are jealous of a title, Jane!"

"Of course I am!" Jane said with a laugh. "What woman wouldn't want to be a duchess? And with a duke that looks like that?"

Marie tried not to show Jane just how surprised she was at her words. They had always been close friends, and Jane had been nothing but fully supportive of whatever Marie was feeling toward her current marital state. Therefore, she should be as irked as Marie. Though ... perhaps she wasn't as reluctant as she had been previously.

It was fairly early this Christmas morning, and they were ensconced in the library as they waited for the day's festivities to begin. There would be church this evening before Christmas dinner, of course, but first, the party had decided to enjoy all that the winter had to offer with a walk outdoors through the lush evergreens of Hollyvale.

"So," said Jane with some encouragement, as she looked around to ensure no one lingered nearby. "Has something happened? You *did* look particularly close as you danced last evening."

Marie fiddled with her gown as she tried to decide what she should tell Jane. She was one of her greatest friends, and yet what was between her and Lionel seemed like it should be private.

"Oh, Jane," she sighed, finally. "I don't know what to think. I am normally very sure of myself, of my desires and my decisions, but he makes me so entirely confused. I find myself beginning to think that marriage to the man would not be as particularly awful as I used to believe."

"What about what Harry said? About his ... proclivities for other women, other activities? His desire to take other woman outside of the marriage bed?"

Marie was silent for a moment. Jane spoke aloud the root of all that was holding her back from giving more of her heart to Lionel. Did he still feel the same, now that he knew her? He had spoken of it last night but had not made any promises.

"I don't know, Jane," she whispered. "I want to hope that if we were married, he would no longer consider other women, but perhaps I wouldn't be enough for him. It doesn't help that I find myself inexplicably attracted to him, but I wonder if this is all a game to him. I want to know that he feels something for me in return before I give him my heart, or else I am bound to spend the rest of my days simply longing for the man who remains out of my grasp."

"Do you think he feels anything for you?"

Marie's cheeks warmed, but she kept her gaze forward.

"I believe he feels ... something, but I am not entirely sure the extent of it. He has made clear that he desires me, that is for certain. I am afraid, however..."

"Of what?"

"I am afraid that once he has me — really has me, he will no longer care anything for me at all." Her words came out in a rush as she voiced what concerned her the most.

"But you will be his wife!" Jane exclaimed.

"Yes," she responded, "though I am not sure of what difference that will make to him."

Marie's palms became clammy as she remembered their conversation regarding the matter — and not only the words, but what it had led to afterward. He had wanted to prove that he cared. But did his actions mean he cared about *her*, Marie Colemore, or simply about her body? He had been selfless, not finding his own satisfaction, and yet.... She sighed. In the end, did it really matter? The worst part of it all was that the more she about it, the more it did.

LIONEL WHISTLED a tune as he sauntered down the corridor to the library, where they were to congregate before leaving on their Christmas Day walk. He wasn't sure who all would be in attendance, but when he had asked Marie if she was going, she replied, "of course," with a strange look on her face that told him he should not have even bothered asking. So here he was.

He had hardly slept at all last night, so caught up he was in everything Marie. Her looks, her smell, her taste. They could be married no matter her opinion on the subject, for without a doubt she would do as her father wished. But he refused to have an unwilling wife. Now he intended to convince her that he could be a man worthy of her.

"Something — or someone — seems to have you in rather good spirits."

Lionel was pulled out of his thoughts by Whitby, who was approaching from the hallway. The cloak over his arm was similar to that which Lionel carried in anticipation of the outdoors.

"It's Christmas, Whitby," he replied. "Is it not a day to celebrate?"

"I've seen you on Christmas before, and you have never looked like this," Whitby said, an eyebrow arched. "I had thought you would be trying to escape by now, but instead you seem to be enjoying yourself. Has the girl caught your attention, then?"

"You could say that," Lionel responded with a shrug as they entered the room, not wanting to say more about his relationship with Marie.

It was a lively group that greeted them, and amongst many Christmas greetings, they began to assemble to head outdoors. Lionel walked to the windows, looking out over the scene before him. The snow fell in huge, heavy chunks landing upon the blankets of snowbanks that stretched across what he knew underneath were grassy meadows, to the small fence post and the grove of trees reaching to the sky behind it.

"Happy Christmas, all!" Marie's brother called out with a

clap of his hands. "We have been blessed with snow this Christmas, and I have a proposition for you. A walk seems somewhat ... boring. What do you say we begin a game outdoors? Blind man's Buff, anyone?"

Marie apparently wasn't the only one in the family with a competitive spirit and love for games and the like. As the party agreed with the viscount, Lionel caught up to Marie as they stepped through the library's garden doors and into the fresh air.

When she wouldn't look at him, instead keeping her gaze straight forward, Lionel smiled. She didn't know what to say to him after last night, he figured, and he reached down and sought her gloved hand.

"Are you all right?" he whispered in her ear after bending down to her so softly and silently that she jumped in surprise when his breath brushed her skin.

"I am, yes, thank you," she said, and a thrill of pleasure coursed through him with the knowledge that he could affect her in such a way. Today she wore a deep blue dress that was meant for walking or riding, he was sure, as her skirts were much less pronounced. She had carried a scarlet cloak on her arm, and now she shook it out as she prepared to toss it around her shoulders.

"Allow me," he said, purposely allowing the backs of his fingers to brush against her long, elegant neck.

"Thank you," she murmured, and they stepped outside into the chilled air. The yard apparently had been cleared earlier in the day, but already the bare spots were beginning to become covered in patches of snow.

His new friend Burrton was to be the first to wear the buff, and the man agreed amiably enough. Lionel regretted that he had to leave Marie's side, but soon they were scampering around the yard with the rest of them, laughing and shouting at one another when the time was right, but also remaining silent so as not to be caught by the blindfolded Burrton. They had decided he had to catch every one of them before passing on the buff to the next person, whoever was unlucky enough to be his first catch.

Lionel was one of the first caught, but he didn't much care. For despite his athletic prowess, he couldn't concentrate on the game, so busy he was watching Marie. He admired her stealth and quickness. In fact, she was nearly athletic as he, though in an entirely different way. She easily dodged Burrton, used other players as a distraction, and before long she was the only one left in the game. She said nothing when she was declared the winner, though Lionel didn't miss the self-satisfied smile she wore as she watched him take the buff from Burrton.

He held out the piece of cloth toward her.

"Will you do the honors, Lady Marie?"

She inclined her head. "I suppose."

When she came up behind him, he closed his eyes so he could better sense her — her heady scent of jasmine, the touch of her hands near the back of his head. Lionel had never felt more fortunate that he chose not to wear a wig nor powder his hair — he could much better feel her fingers in his queue.

"There we are, your grace," she said as she tied the knot firmly. "Best of luck."

"I'll be needing it," he said with a low chuckle.

His words proved presumptuous, however, as he was rather proficient at the game once he tuned into his other senses. He found Lovell first, followed by a couple of the ladies. Once again, one person remained elusive.

"Marie, you've won again, dash it all," he heard Lovell say, and Lionel took off the buff.

"She should have played for the cricket team at Eton!" he said with a laugh, and while the others joined in the merriment, he looked around in vain for the woman in question, the one person whose expression met the most.

"Where *is* Lady Marie?" he asked Lovell.

"She was standing right here a moment ago," Lovell answered with a shrug. "She's likely hiding somewhere nearby."

"Surely she didn't try to cheat the game," Lionel said, hands on his hips.

"No, she wouldn't," mused Lovell. "I'm sure she'll appear in a moment or so."

Lionel nodded, though when the game began again, he became somewhat concerned. He noticed that not only Marie was missing, but Downe as well. He left the yard, which constituted the game space, and began to look around the perimeter.

"Marie?" he called out a couple of times into the wooded area beyond.

"Over here!" he finally heard her call, and with some relief he followed her voice, finding her next to a tree, with Downe standing beside her, his arms crossed. He certainly looked perturbed that Lionel had come across them.

Marie seemed annoyed, relief crossing her face as Lionel approached. He turned his attention to Downe, and while he spoke to Marie, he kept his gaze upon the man. "Is everything all right, Lady Marie?"

"All is fine now," she said with a nod. "Though may I speak to you for a moment?"

"Of course."

When Downe remained, she added, "Alone?"

"Right," said Downe, though when he shot Lionel a self-satisfied smile as he walked away, Lionel couldn't help but be somewhat worried at what had occurred in the few moments they had been alone.

"Is everything actually all right?" he repeated, and now she hugged her arms around herself as she looked from one side to the other, though the others in their party, while visible through the trees, was nowhere near enough to hear.

"Yes," she replied softly. "I just wanted a moment alone without him. He was ... suggesting things he had no business to."

"I see," Lionel said, his jaw setting tightly. "Why don't we go for a walk?"

"All right." She took his offered arm and began to lead them through the trees.

8

"Your family's grounds are impressive," Lionel said as they meandered along the snowy path. He allowed Marie to lead the way, as familiar as she was with the area.

"You should see it in the spring and summer," she said wistfully. "My mother takes great pride in its upkeep."

"Does she retain any connections to France?" he asked, curious regarding the family's relations to the country. They were at peace now, but it was all still fairly new after the years of war.

"None at all," she said, shaking her head. "Did your father not tell you of my family?"

"I'm sure he did, but I must admit I can't remember much. I was a boy and didn't know at the time how our lives would intertwine."

"Oh. Well. During the conflict when my mother was quite young, her parents left France for England. My grandfather was actually British himself, and they had always been sympathetic to the country. Anyway, she hardly remembers France at all. In fact, I'm not sure she even speaks the language anymore."

"That would be a shame," he said. "It's a beautiful language. Do you speak it?"

"I do." She nodded. "Though I was primarily taught by a governess."

They were silent for a moment before he continued. "Would you like to tell me of what Downe said to you?"

"Simply that I could be much happier with a man like him. A man who would put me first, make me his one and only woman. He said he would worship the ground at my feet."

"Did he, now?"

"He did."

"And do you believe him?"

"I suppose in a way I do," she said, and his stomach began to churn. "He has certainly been persistent in his attention toward me. But I'm not sure of the *way* in which he would admire me, if that makes sense?"

"I believe so."

At least Marie was a smart woman.

"Anyway, I told him that I am to be married soon, and I asked that he not make such comments again. Then you came upon us at a most opportune moment."

Lionel stopped sharply and turned her toward him. "Were you concerned he would try to force himself upon you?"

"No, of course not," she said with a small smile in a blatant attempt to reassure him. "I've known him for years of course, as Jane's brother. He's harmless. Just annoying."

"Annoying he is," Lionel murmured, though the spark of anger within him continued to burn.

"Please leave it alone, Lionel," Marie said, apparently

reading his thoughts. "There is no need to say anything to him."

"Very well," he replied, though this was not the type of thing he could just leave. He would certainly be having a conversation — at the very least — with the man.

"Where are we at the moment?" he asked, taking in their surroundings. All of it was beginning to look the same.

"You don't recognize the pond?" she asked, turning a smile upon him. "This is where we went skating yesterday."

He looked around, realizing that the ice had been covered with snow overnight. The untouched snow practically sparkled as it stretched out before them.

"Do you fancy another race, Marie?" he asked, and she turned to him with eyebrows raised.

"We don't have skates — nor ice, at the moment."

"Can you not run?"

For a moment, her eyes lit up as though she wanted to agree, but then they quickly became hooded.

"We shouldn't," she said.

"Why? Because it's not ladylike?"

"Not in the least!"

"No one will know."

"You will."

"That I will. And I would applaud you for it."

She chewed her lip as she thought about his words.

"Fine," she finally said. "Just one race — and do *not* tell a soul. Especially my mother."

"You have my word."

He grinned at her then drew a line in the snow with his foot.

"One ... two ... three ... Go!"

He began a quick jog, allowing her to keep even with him, but when she broke away despite her skirts flapping around her legs, he picked up his pace. His long legs were much more equipped to traverse the foot-high snow, and soon enough he had pulled away and was approaching the tree line, which was their agreed-upon finish. He looked for Marie, turning around to watch her struggling through the deepening snow.

"Not fair!" she called and laughed at her.

"Would you like a rematch?"

"Of course! I—"

Her words cut off and resounded in a scream. One moment she had been running toward him, and in the next, she had simply disappeared.

"Marie?" he shouted, his heart pounding as he raced back toward her. "Marie!"

He knew but seconds had passed as he sprinted to her, but somehow they felt like hours. When he finally came upon her, he breathed out a huge sigh of relief as she was still floating above the icy water, her hands desperately trying to grasp the jagged borders of ice around her.

"Lionel!" she gasped, and her lips already turning blue. "I can't ... I can't hold on much longer. I'm so ... heavy ... in this dress."

Lionel sat down on his arse, his boots astride hole. He grabbed her hands, dug his heels in, and with one strong pull, yanked her up on top of him. He said a prayer of thanks for how light yet strong she was as they both lay gasping in the snow.

"Marie," he said once they both caught their breath. "We have to move or you'll freeze to death. We must be careful — with the warmer temperatures, the new snow's weight must have weakened the ice.

She nodded, and they slowly began making their way to land, as Lionel tested each step before putting his weight down. It was an agonizingly slow progress forward, but it was better than both of them falling in, completely alone with no one around to help.

"We're ... on ... the shore," Marie gasped, and Lionel couldn't think of a time when he had ever before felt so relieved.

He swung Marie into his arms and began the journey back to the house. It wasn't far, though every time he looked up at Hollyvale, it seemed as though it was retreating into the distance. Marie shivered in his arms, causing him to increase his pace, his boots now completely soaked as he trudged through the snow. *Stupid*, he berated himself. *I should have known better. The weather slightly warmed, a heavy snow had fallen. This is my fault.*

As they neared the house, Marie stirred in his arms, lifting her head to look at the manor in front of them.

"Go through the servants' entrance," she said shakily, and at his look of consternation, she gave him a small nod, as if to tell him that now was not the time to disagree with him.

He did as she said, as much to appease her wishes as due to the fact that they were approaching the back of the manor and the servants' entrance was closer. Not wanting to put Marie down, he used his boot to knock on the door, and it swung open shortly to reveal the housekeeper.

"My goodness!" she gasped, ushering them in. "Lady Marie, what has happened?"

"She fell through the ice," Lionel told her hurriedly, not wanting to stop in his haste to get her somewhere warm. "Can you show me the way to her room?"

"Aye, your grace," the woman said, calling to another young girl to fetch Marie's lady's maid.

He followed the housekeeper through the maze of corridors until they finally stopped before a door. The house-keeper let him in, looking mildly concerned, likely due to the fact he was in a lady's bedroom, but he didn't overly care at the moment.

He deposited Marie on the bed, beginning to peel off her cloak. The housekeeper made a slight noise behind him, but he silenced her with a glare before turning back and resuming his progress. He wasn't going to allow Marie to freeze to death due to propriety. He had just undone the row of buttons at the back of her gown when her maid came rushing in. Marie sat up at her voice and waved a hand in the air at the three concerned faces looking down at her.

"I'm fine," she said, teeth chattering. "Just a mite cold."

Lionel ensured the lady's maid and the housekeeper had everything well in hand before walking over and adding logs to the fire so that it burned with gusto in the hearth before he left. He took one last long look behind him as he approached the door.

"I will be back to check on you shortly," he said, and she simply nodded at him before helping her maid slide the sleeves of her dress down. Everything within him wanted to stay, to be there himself to make sure she was all right, but there was no way he could, not when others knew of his presence here. And so he contented himself with knowing she was in good hands and he could remain nearby, and shut the door softly behind him.

9

Oh heavens, but she was cold.

Marie huddled even deeper into the down blankets piled upon her as she pulled her wrapper tighter around herself. She had already taken a warm bath and endured a visit with her mother, who was hopeful that Marie would still be able to make the church service and dinner that evening. Marie promised that if she had warmed enough, she would do her very best.

She was sinking back into her bed, content but relaxed, when there came another soft knock on the door.

"Hello?" she called as the door eased open a crack, and she was surprised when Lionel filled the entrance.

"May I come in?" he asked in his deep voice, the one that sent shivers down her spine.

"Um…" She chewed her lip. "I suppose, as long as no one has seen you."

"I can assure you that I have been as stealthy as a spy," he said, causing her to laugh.

She raised her eyebrows when he came in and took a seat on the bed beside her instead of in the nearby chair.

"Are you well?" he asked.

"I feel completely fine," she said with all honesty. "Except for the fact that I am chilled down to my very bones and no matter what I do I cannot seem to get warm."

He took her hand in his, his gaze upon her long fingers as his big hands warmed her, and she wished they could warm her entire body.

"I'm sorry, Marie," he said softly. "This was entirely my fault. I should have known better. I—"

"Stop," she said, holding up a hand. "You cannot blame yourself — not at all. If anyone should have known better, it was me. In fact ... I wanted to thank you."

He looked up at her, and she enjoyed the feel of his dark blue eyes seemingly caressing her, for once with complete focus as they roved her face, apparently appraising her wellbeing.

"For what?"

"For being there for me. For bringing me home so quickly. For being so fast and so strong. For caring." She smiled as she said it, her lips widening as she took in his incredulity.

"Of course I care," he said, the pressure of his hands increasing. "I care very much."

She leaned up then and took his strong chin in between her hands. She looked over his face, at his thick, full eyebrows, his prominent cheekbones and the square jaw that she held in her hands. She couldn't help herself. She wanted him with a ferocity she could no longer ignore.

Marie pulled him down toward her, sitting up to meet him halfway as she brought her lips to his. His responding kiss was firm, in follow up to his words. One of his hands came behind her head, the other to the back of her body as he held her upright. He was so strong, she thought as his tongue entered her mouth, tangled in a love play with hers. And he was so warm. She let him pull her in closer, her hands coming over his shoulders now as she sought his closeness, stealing his body heat from him, and his arms tightened around her.

She pushed back the blankets, wanting nothing between them, and within moments, she was straddling his lap, though she felt no reservations now, nothing but a desperation for more. More of him, more of the sensations coursing through her.

He had changed his clothing, she noted through her clouded thoughts, and she broke away from his kiss to bring her lips to his neck and up to his ear, tasting and teasing him as he held her with his broad hands around her waist.

She needed to feel him, to know what he would be like against her fingertips, and she clumsily untied his cravat, throwing it to the side. She brought her hands to his neck, his skin hot as her fingers came lower, working at the buttons of his waistcoat until that joined the cravat on the floor.

"Marie," he groaned, but now she was on a mission, her actions frenzied, hurried. She undid the buttons of his linen shirt, and he now helped her, wresting his arms out. She stilled for a moment, leaning back and appreciating the hard lines of his torso, the thick muscles that bulged in his shoulders and biceps.

She now divested herself of her wrapper, and heat radiated off him, seeping into her through her thin chemise, the only thing that now separated them. Finally, warmth began to course through her body, replacing the icy chill that had settled in.

"Marie," Lionel ground out, his voice radiating tension.

"I cannot hold myself back from you any longer. I either leave now or…"

"Or."

He groaned and, no longer holding himself back, he took control, loosening the fall of his breeches and sliding them off before divesting her of her chemise. He laid her back on the bed, pulling the blankets over both of them, and she was grateful to be cocooned in the warmth that enveloped them.

He kissed her again, his practiced lips and tongue sliding over hers, and she didn't know what came over her as she lifted her hips to him, moving in a rhythm she seemed to instinctively already know.

She brought his hand to her breast, wanting to feel the same thrill course through her as she had before. He seemed to have no issue with appeasing her, and soon he was pressed hard against her stomach.

"Lionel," she whispered. "Please … now…"

No longer did she feel any bit of coldness. Instead, he had set her body on flame and she wanted more, to burn until she exploded.

"Are you sure?" His voice was ragged, the pain apparent in his question but she appreciated him for it all the same.

"Yes," she murmured, and then he was there at her entrance, slowly easing himself inside of her. She gasped as he filled her, his thickness stretching her. He paused for a moment before pushing forward. She winced at the bit of pain that sliced through her, and he stilled for a moment, bringing his forehead to hers, kissing her soundly enough to distract her. His ploy worked. Soon enough, she was moving against him once more, and he took his cue from her and began to thrust.

The glorious sensations began to build inside her, and

she became frenzied, desperate for the release that she now knew was possible.

"Come for me, Marie," he murmured, and she did as he commanded, explosions rocking her and convulsing through her body. She was so overcome that she hardly noticed what happened next, but he must have found his own release as he soon collapsed, rolling off of her and hugging her to his side in nearly one fluid motion.

"My goodness," she said in awe. "I never knew just how … wonderful that could be."

He chuckled as he pulled her in tighter. "I'm glad you enjoyed it, love," he said.

She could practically feel her heart glowing through her chest. *Did he call me love? Did he mean it?* For, against her better judgment, despite how she had tried to distance herself, she could no longer deny the feelings she had for him, nor how much she wanted him to care for her equally. Did she *love* him? It was hard to know so soon, but she had certainly never felt such a depth of emotion before.

"Did I warm you up?" he asked, his breath tickling her ear as he asked her.

"I should say so." She chuckled, no longer suffering any bit of cold, but rather heated right through.

There came a sudden knock and they both jumped slightly.

"Yes?" Marie called as Lionel stilled behind her.

"My lady? Your mother sent me to ask if you would like to join in this evening's festivities. Can I help you prepare?"

"Ah — yes, Lydia, I will be attending, but could you return in a few minutes?"

"Of course, my lady."

Marie practically pushed Lionel from her bed, frowning at his laughter.

"It's not funny!" she protested as she pulled her night-gown back over her head. "We could have been found out and then what would have happened?"

"We would have been married," he said with a shrug. "Nothing would have changed but, perhaps, the wedding's timing."

"And our reputations would have been ruined!"

"For the near future," he said nonchalantly. "Soon enough everyone would forget and all would be well."

She shook her head at him.

"I am not sure if I will ever understand you."

He grinned wolfishly at her. "But isn't it fun to try?"

She swatted his arm. "Get your clothes on before Lydia comes back," she said. "Despite your lack of care, I would prefer not to be caught with you in here and have to explain to my parents."

"And my mother," he added, grinning at her. "Don't forget she is joining us this evening."

"Oh, of course, how could I forget?" she asked, inwardly cringing, as she certainly had forgotten the woman would be arriving tonight.

"Now, Marie, do I detect some hesitation in your tone?"

"Not at all," she said, willing him to dress faster. She got off the bed herself and began helping him with his clothes, crouching to tie up his falls.

"Careful, love," he said looking down at her. "You might start something again."

"Oh, you ... you...." She shook her head, unable to find the words. Then she stood and pointed to the door. "Out you go!"

When he remained where he was, she opened the door a crack and peered out into the hall. Finding it empty, she grabbed his elbow, led him over, and pushed him out while he was still doing up his waistcoat.

"Happy Christmas," he said as he slipped out the door with one last grin.

"Happy Christmas," she said, trying to hide her laugh before shutting the door behind him and sagging against it. She should feel like a harlot, filled with remorse over her actions. It was far from the truth, however. For all that filled her was an intense satisfaction, and a wish to do it all over again.

10

Lionel had not attended a church service in ... well, years, he realized with some surprise. However, if Marie was going to church tonight, then he would as well. Besides that, his mother had just arrived and there was no chance he was going to leave the two of them alone together. They were both strong-willed females, and he didn't want to admit how nervous he was for the two of them to be alone.

"Darling," his mother said as she walked in the door, her arms coming around him in the requisite embrace, though it was difficult to feel any comfort in it when the beading upon her jacket felt as though it was stabbing him. "Happy Christmas," she said with a tight-lipped smile as she looked past him and around the great hall into the foyer, where all had gathered before leaving for church.

"Happy Christmas, Mother."

"You look well."

"As do you."

Their stilted greetings finished, he heard murmurs behind him, and he turned to see Marie slowly descending the stairs, her gold and green gown trailing on the steps behind her. The woman certainly knew how to dress, he thought, as he took in the matching hat tipped jauntily on her head, showcasing her luxurious dark curls. He thought of them cascading through his fingers but an hour or two earlier, and he swallowed hard as he tried to push the thoughts away.

He was drawn to her side when she reached the bottom stair, his arm extending in offering to him. She took it, looking up at him with a smile reserved for a lover.

"Marie," her brother said, joining them with a worried look on his face. "Are you well? I know Mother pushed you to attend this evening, but you know how she is. If you want to stay behind—"

"I'm fine," she said, placing a hand on his arm. "Thank you, Ned, for your concern, but I am considerably warmed."

Lionel coughed.

"I'm glad to hear it," her brother said. If only he knew the particulars, he might not be so pleased. "Now, we must be off or we will be late."

They filed through the door to begin the short walk to the village church. Lionel was so focused on Marie that he had forgotten his mother until she joined him on his other side.

"Lady Catherine," Marie said, peering around him. "How lovely to see you again. I am so pleased that you were able to join us this evening."

"Yes, well," his mother said with a sniff. "I would have preferred staying at Lady Panmore's house party, but Lionel insisted on attending this party instead of joining me there — and of course, I wanted to be near him on Christmas. So here I am."

"I hope you shall enjoy tonight's service."

"I'm sure it will be very ... provincial."

Lionel glanced at Marie out of the corner of his eye, and he could tell the smile she wore on her face was forced.

"Mother," he said, sending a look of warning her way.

"Yes, darling?"

"Lord St. James and his family have been very welcoming, and I am rather enjoying my time here. I am sure you will do the same."

"Yes, dear," she said with such sarcasm Lionel wanted to roll his eyes. "I am sure that I will."

OH, the woman was as abominable as Marie remembered. She sniffed throughout the entire church service, as though she was above them all, and when it was time to walk home, she took Lionel's arm, leaving Marie to walk behind them. When Lord Downe came up beside her and held out his elbow, she bristled, and she saw Lionel look over his shoulder with concern. She could tell he was going to leave his mother's side to join her, but she gave him a slight shake of her head. They were amongst their entire party, and she could handle the man for the short walk. No need to cause his mother further consternation.

"Might I say how beautiful you look tonight, Lady Marie?" Lord Downe said, bending his head much closer to her than was necessary.

"That is very kind of you, Lord Downe," she said, keeping her spine stiff straight as she leaned back slightly away from him.

"It is a pity that you do it all for a man who does not appreciate you," he said in a low voice.

"I do not wish to have this conversation."

"About the Duke of Ware," he said, raising his eyebrows. "Did my sister not tell you of his ... proclivities? I realize that there has been a longstanding arrangement for the two of you to be married, but the man never wanted a wife, as he would tell all who would listen. I despair the thought of a woman like you trapped in a marriage with a man of such depravity."

"You lie," she said, giving him a look as frosty as the night around them. "I have come to know the duke, and while I do not know much of his past, he has proven to be quite considerate and attentive toward me."

"For now," Lord Downe said with a shrug. "But in the future? He will tire of you. Men such as him always do."

"You do not know him well enough, then," she said, wanting him to stop speaking to her, needing to defend Lionel, and yet at the same time fearful that there was an ounce of truth to his words. For Lionel had told her on their initial meeting that he foresaw a marriage where he found his pleasure outside of the marriage bed. She was assuming all of that had changed along with their growing closeness, but what if she was wrong? Was she a fool who had allowed him to charm her into giving him what he wanted? Would he now be on his way to find another?

No, Marie. Do not allow Lord Downe to question your intuition.

"Say what you want, Lord Downe," she said with all the disdain she could muster. "You will not come between the two of us. *That* I can promise you."

Relief coursed through her as Hollyvale came into sight.

"When I am proven right, Lady Marie," he said with a sneer, "then know that I continue to have feelings for you, and would gladly court you myself."

She nodded but dropped his arm, unwilling to touch the

vile man any longer, even through layers of garments. Whether what he said was true or not, his intentions certainly weren't the noble sort.

"Oh, and Marie?"

"*Lady* Marie."

"Can you really call yourself that? Know that I am the only gentleman who *will* have you once all learn that you are no longer an innocent."

She stopped still then, frozen, as she looked at him in horror. He only laughed and continued on his way, and someone bumped into Marie's back. How had he known? Surely, Lionel wouldn't have said anything. The most sickening thought, however, was whether Lord Downe was right. She had only truly known her betrothed for a couple of days, despite how close they had become in such a short time. Was she really just another conquest?

Well, she was determined to find out.

LIONEL WASN'T sure why Marie seemed somewhat perturbed with him through the Christmas dinner, though he had a suspicion it had something to do with Downe. He should have followed his intuition and not allowed the man even a moment walking with her alone.

Over courses of cheese, soup, minced pies, frumetnery with venison, and plum pudding, Lionel continued to eye Marie across the table. She seemed well recovered from her ordeal earlier in the day, thank goodness, though he thought she was looking a little tired. What in the hell was wrong with him? He shook his head. Never in his life had he paid such attention to every little movement made by another person, let alone a woman.

But Marie was different. He knew that in his heart. And when he saw the way she eyed him with something like suspicion, a niggling worry began in his stomach. Did she regret what they had done this afternoon? He should have waited — he knew better — but when she had continued to ask him for his love, he could no longer deny her.

Was his mother the cause of Marie's vexation? She was currently droning on and on beside him, but he had stopped listening about four courses ago. His eye began to tic, an old habit that usually only she brought out.

"It's a very fine meal, Mother," he finally snapped at her after she continued to criticize dish after dish, her voice in his ear purposefully just loud enough, he knew, for many of their dinner companions to hear.

"Lionel!" she exclaimed with some surprise. "Why must you speak so harshly to me — your own mother?"

He sighed, and turned back to his plate, his focus remaining across the table at Marie. She was unusually quiet.

"Lady Marie," he finally said, and she looked up at him with wide eyes. "Are you well?"

"I am, your grace," she said with the utmost politeness. "I suppose I am just tired."

"That's understandable."

"Oh yes, I heard of your unfortunate mishap," his mother said from beside him. "Tell me, my dear, why in heaven's name would you go walking on thin ice? Do you not know your own property better than that? Why, my Lionel could have gone through as well, and then what would happen to us all?"

Marie's eyes narrowed, and she opened her mouth to retort, but Lionel held up a hand in an attempt to keep the peace.

"Mother," he said, keeping his tone even. "Lady Marie and I went for a walk, that is all. In fact, we were all skating on the ice yesterday and there were no warning signs. It was an unfortunate occurrence, and we are all relieved that Lady Marie has suffered no ill effects."

"Mmm hmm," she said with the sniff that she was famous for, and Lionel groaned, wishing this dinner was over. He wanted nothing more than for his mother to show Marie some respect, as soon enough they would all be living as one. Having the two forceful women in the same home did not bode well for the future. Especially his future. Not at all.

11

Despite her best intentions, Marie could not stop thinking about Lord Downe's words. Throughout dinner, they played round in her head, as did the future lying ahead of her with the woman she would soon call mother-in-law. Never in her life had Marie come second to anyone, and she was determined that it would certainly not be that way with her husband.

She finally had a moment alone with Lionel after dinner, when the men joined them in the drawing room. She drew him off to the side, into an alcove just down the corridor. A sculpture in front of them shielded them somewhat from view, though she turned her back to the room so that her angry glare would not be shared with the rest of them.

He was leaning against the curved silk-wallpapered wall behind him, arms crossed over his chest as he looked her up and down.

"Well, Marie?" he asked. "I can tell something is on your mind. I would sorely love to hear it rather than this continued coldness you are presenting toward me."

She took a deep breath and steeled her resolve.

"The night we met, you heard what Jane told me about your ... activities. I have been told more about them, and I also recall our conversation regarding our marriage. How I would perhaps be ... sharing you with other women. If I have not yet been clear enough, I would like to make certain you understand me, Lionel. I will not share. If you want me, you have me alone, and I will not agree to any other arrangement. Is that clear?"

He smiled slightly, though showed no other emotion, and she wasn't sure whether he was mocking her or not. "You make yourself very clear, Marie."

"Good," she responded, rocking back and forth from the toes to the heels of her thin gold slippers. "So is it true?"

She swallowed hard, not sure if she wanted to hear his response.

"Is what true?"

"His accusations. That you spend all your time in a brothel. That you did not want a wife. That you enjoy ... depravity."

He pushed back from the wall, coming to stand in front of her, his feet wide apart. "Do you believe it to be true?"

Her lower lip began to tremble, and she caught it between her teeth.

"I really don't know," she said, then folded her arms in front of her as she tried to gather strength. "But I won't have it."

"Oh you won't, will you?"

"No," she said, her jaw tightening. "You will refrain from ever visiting such a place again, nor even speaking to such women."

"My, you are a bossy one," he said, and she noticed a slight tic beside his right eye. "If you really need to know,

76

Marie, I have frequented a brothel a time or two in the past, yes. But it is not as your Lord Downe says. I have no depravities to speak of, and I am not extremely pleased you didn't believe me the first time I told you. In fact, Lord Downe may very well be describing himself in his words to you and unfortunately has brought his poor sister into his lies. You need not fear indiscretions from me, Marie. But," he continued, "I am not pleased that you think so poorly of me. And I will not be told what to do by my wife. Do you understand?"

Marie wasn't sure whether to fight him back on this or to nod and agree. For there was a very good chance he was right — it was Lord Downe's word against his. But she didn't like the way he questioned her, didn't want to agree to his terms. She would tell him how she damn well felt, she thought, stomping her heel into the ground, then wincing as there was nothing to pad it from the floor at her feet.

"There's one more thing," she said. "Something of even greater consequence."

"Oh?"

"Lord Downe suggested he knew that I was no longer an innocent, that you and I had ... well..."

"Do you really think I would tell anyone of what we did together this afternoon?" he asked, his eyebrows coming together as he stared at her in consternation.

"How else would he know?" she asked, panic beginning to fill her as she wondered who else may be aware of her activities. Did the entire house party know?

"I have no idea," he responded with a sigh. "The servants? I am not sure, Marie, but you simply have to deny it, and no one can prove a thing. More importantly, you must also begin thinking better of me. If I am to be your husband, we must trust one another."

"Agreed," she said with a soft sigh, but her heart was

heavy as they returned to the drawing room, an unspoken tension simmering between them.

WHEN MARIE ROSE the next morning, she pulled back the heavy curtain of her windows to gaze out on Hollyvale's snow-covered grounds below. She had always loved the sun's reflection glinting off the white snow, untouched by footprints or human hand. When she was a girl, she had loved running out into the woods, watching her feet make an imprint, as though she were scratching the first lines of charcoal onto a sketch pad.

It was not to be today, however. No, she was to be a hostess today, and she and her mother would be entertaining Lady Catherine in the breakfast room as they discussed her upcoming marriage to Lionel.

She dressed in a pink muslin gown, threw a shawl over her shoulders, and after Lydia tucked her curls together in a knot on the back of her head, she made her way downstairs, smiling at the warmth Christmastide had brought into their home.

Marie was walking down the corridor when she jumped, startled by a sudden presence waiting in the arch of a doorway.

"Lady Catherine!" she exclaimed, bringing a hand to her breast as she slowed her breathing. "My apologies. You startled me."

"Apparently."

The woman's gray hair was piled elegantly atop her head, her dress formal even for this simple morning breakfast. Marie wasn't sure if she would ever live up to the image this woman had created — but did she actually want to?

78

"Is something amiss, Lady Catherine?" she asked, as the woman continued to stare at her, her eyes narrowing.

"I heard something last evening which has greatly distressed me," she said in her raspy voice.

"I am sorry to hear that," Marie said with what she hoped to be outward calm, although her heart beat rapidly. "Is there anything I can do to help?"

"Yes," she said, stepping toward her, pointing a bony finger at Marie's chest. "You can get yourself away from my son. He is a duke, one of the highest in the realm, and we have no need for you in our lives."

"Excuse me?"

"I know what you did, you nasty girl. You are the daughter of a peer, and yet you give yourself away like a common whore."

Fury rising from deep within Marie, she clenched her fists at her side in order to keep it at bay.

"I am nothing of the sort, Lady Catherine, and I am sorry you feel that way," she said, her words clipped. "But it does not matter what you think of me. For your son wishes to marry me, and he is the duke, is he not?"

"This is true," she said, a sly smile breaking out over her face. "But once I speak with him, I am sure he will want to marry you no more."

Marie paused for a moment, confused at why Lady Catherine telling her son she knew of their coupling would make a difference to him. But, for the moment, she was too overcome with the sneer that had distorted the woman's face.

"Why do you hate me so?" she asked, more curious than anything. She had never done anything to harm Lady Catherine, and — yesterday's activities aside — she should be a good match for Lionel.

"You are just like your mother," the dowager duchess said, her lip curling. "A French harlot."

"Say what you want about me," Marie responded in a low whisper, looking over Lady Catherine's shoulder to see her mother round the corner. She and Marie had certainly had their disagreements, but Marie loved her family with all of her being and she was not going to stand by and let anyone speak poorly of them. "But my mother is a wonderful woman, and you are lucky to be a guest in her home. Now, Lady Catherine, I might suggest that you are too ill to partake in this breakfast. I would not like to see you make such disparaging remarks to my mother's face. Good day to you."

And with that, Marie lifted her head high, brushed by the vile woman, and stalked down the hall toward her mother, taking her arm and giving her Lady Catherine's regards and regrets.

LIONEL WAS in the library playing faro with Whitby and Burrton when he felt a tap on his shoulder. He turned to find the family's butler.

"The Duchess Catherine wishes to see you, your grace," he said in his severe, somber tone.

"Please tell her I will speak to her later this morning," he said, focusing on his cards.

"She said it was urgent, your grace. I apologize."

Lionel turned back to his companions and sighed, folding his cards in front of him. "Well, gentleman, forgive me, but I suppose I must see what the emergency is."

"This isn't a ploy, is it Ware, to back out when you are

losing?" asked Burrton with a chuckle, his hair standing out around his head.

"Not at all," he said, pushing his chair in. "I hope to rejoin you shortly."

He followed the butler into a scarcely used drawing room, finding his mother sitting stiffly in a wingback armchair.

"Oh, Lionel, I am so glad you came," she said, as though she had given him any choice. He took a side chair and flipped it around, straddling it as he faced her. She sniffed and looked at him with disdain, though she didn't say anything.

"It's about that girl," she said, her gaze not on him, but on the wall behind him.

"Marie?"

"Yes, of course," she said, holding tightly to her cane. "I have heard the most distressing news."

"And that would be?"

"The strumpet gave away her innocence! I can hardly believe it, Lionel. How horrible for you!"

He would beg to differ.

"And to that awful Lord Downe! I can hardly believe it, Lionel, you must call off the betrothal *at once*. I should have known that she is just like her mother. Go speak with Hartford and we will be off immediately."

He stared at his mother in shock.

"Lord Downe? And who is Hartford?"

If he hadn't seen it himself, he would never have believed it had happened, but his mother's cheeks turned bright red.

"Did I say Hartford? I meant the Marquess of St. James."

"That seems awfully familiar, Mother," he said, suspicion niggling at him, suspicion he didn't altogether like.

"We knew one another in our youth," she said primly, waving a hand in the air as if it was of no consequence. "He had something of a *tendre* for me, I believe, but then that French strumpet came along and he had eyes only for her."

Lionel stood, his hands coming to his back. It was all beginning to make sense now.

"That's why you have always hated Marie," he said with wonderment, rubbing his right eye where the tic started up, "Because of how you feel about her mother."

Lady Catherine shrugged one shoulder, refusing to answer him.

"But Father and the Marquess were such great friends!"

"Yes, and after Hart— Lord St. James was so foolish, I realized how fortunate I was that a *duke* was interested in me. It all worked out, Lionel, until your father made that idiotic request in his will for you to marry the girl. Really! Well, it is all finished now."

"No, Mother," he said shaking his head. "It is not finished at all."

12

Lionel took the afternoon to try to come to terms with his mother's revelations. He knew, of course, not to believe her preposterous suggestion of Marie with Downe, but what had caused her to believe such a thing? What had really taken him aback was the discovery of her own past. It was as though he had never truly known his mother at all.

And now what? He was to bring home a wife who would live in the same house as his mother, a woman who wanted nothing to do with her? He ran his hand over his face as he looked for Marie, slowing when he heard her voice coming from inside one of the drawing rooms. He lifted his hand to knock but stopped when he heard his name.

"Oh Patty, I just don't know what to do," Marie said, and he pictured her pacing the room as he heard the rustle of her skirts, though he didn't risk a look in through the crack in the door. "He says he cares for me, but I no longer know if I can believe it. I am also now concerned about the seriousness of his regard for me. And I have only truly known him for but a few days in the country! What if we marry and he returns to the brothels in London and I am left alone with his horrific mother in the country? Patricia, I just couldn't bear it."

"You don't know that he would do such a thing," came Lady Lovell's soft reply. "You have allowed Lady Catherine and Lord Downe to sway your feelings. Do not listen to them but to your heart. What is it telling you?"

Lionel had to force himself to take a breath as he awaited her reply. Nothing mattered but Marie's answer. Did she love him? Did she believe in him? For she was right. It had been but days since they had renewed their acquaintance, and yet he knew all he needed to. No longer did he have any desire to spend his nights in gambling hells or with women of no consequence. No longer did he have any wish to run from his responsibilities of taking a wife or seeing to his own estates. He wanted Marie Colemore. But she needed to feel the same for him.

"I—" He heard her begin. "I—"

But her words were lost when he felt a hand at his shoulder.

"Ware! Good to see you, man. We were just about to begin a new game of whist in the library. Care to join?"

Burrton! Damn the man. Now, not only would he not hear Marie's response, but she was likely fully aware that he had been lurking outside the door, listening to her conversation. That would certainly not grant him any higher esteem in her eyes.

"Sure, Burrton," he muttered. "Lead the way."

MARIE COULD HARDLY BELIEVE IT. Listening to her private conversations from behind closed doors! Could the man not speak directly to her face? She wouldn't have it, she seethed, as she paced her bedroom while preparing for dinner. Not at all.

"Men!" she said, throwing her hands up in the air. "How vexing they are, Lydia!"

Her maid looked at her with wide eyes, unaware of the details of which she was speaking, though she likely knew more than she let on. Servants always did.

"Is there anything I can do, my lady?"

"No," she said with a sigh, flinging herself back on the bed. "Nothing at all."

Two hours later, when she entered the drawing room with her head high and her beautiful navy gown flowing around her feet, she steeled her resolve and told herself to not show the bloody man any emotion until he explained himself. Even then, she would be the judge of whether or not he was worthy of forgiveness. She had to admit, however, that it was now Lionel himself but his mother who caused her the most aggravation. She needed now to determine the true nature of their marriage before she gave her heart to him. Well ... any more of her heart.

For, as she looked at Lionel across the room, in his tight tan breeches, his broad shoulders filling his black, unadorned jacket, and his slightly unfashionable wild hair tied back in its queue, she knew she was falling in love with him. Even now, he was tossing his head back in a laugh, a true laugh, unconcerned over what others around him might think. He lived his life with abandon, and she yearned for that same sense of freedom.

But first, she had to determine if he would ever truly be hers.

She took a step into the room and paused when his head turned to her, the intensity of his eyes arresting her on the spot. He began to walk toward her when she heard the clink of a glass.

"Good evening everyone!" her father's voice boomed. "I hope you are all having a very happy Christmas. We are so glad you could join us. This evening is to be one of particular celebration. Not only are we all here together in this season of gladness, but my daughter, Marie, the loveliest woman I have ever laid eyes upon — besides my wife, of course — is to be married."

Marie gasped at his words. Why in heaven's name was he saying all of this now? This was a private conversation, not one to be had in front of all the guests. She took a step toward him but stilled when Lionel's hand came to her arm. "Just a moment," he murmured.

"You all are likely aware that she has been betrothed to the Duke of Ware for some time now. I am pleased that we have become much closer to the duke throughout this house party, and due to his own request, we will be having the wedding here before the week is through!"

The Marquess of St. James took a drink to that, as did the other guests. Everyone except Marie.

Her pulse pounded, her hands sweated, and she could feel the hairs on her arms rise as her ire did.

"What is the meaning of this?" she hissed through teeth clenched in a smile, and Lionel looked at her with confusion etched on his face.

"I wanted to show you how much I truly wanted to marry you, to be your husband," he said. "Your father agreed to secure a special license."

She took his elbow and all but dragged him from the room, pretending to all who were watching that she was simply in such wonderful spirits that she wanted a moment alone with her dear husband-to-be. When they reached the hall, she whirled him around and pushed him back against the wall so hard he jumped.

"I do not like surprises, Lionel!" she said holding a finger in the air as she paced five steps forward and five steps back in front of him. "Not at all. And this, well, this is something else entirely. I am well aware that I lack a choice as to whether or not I marry you, but within a *week*? Did you not consider that having a proper wedding might matter to me?"

His jaw dropped as though he were flabbergasted that she would even suggest a thing.

"Look, Lionel," she said, her voice softening. "I realize that you were wanting to make a gesture for me, and I do appreciate it. But this is not the way to go about it. Besides that, there are matters of importance to discuss."

"Such as..."

"Your mother, for one. Her disgust for me and my family, as well as the fact that both she and Lord Downe knew of our ... our ..."

"Lovemaking?" he supplied.

"Yes," she said, looking around to make sure no one had heard. "Why would you tell anyone about that? Do you truly care so little that you would ruin my reputation without another thought?"

"Not at all!" he said, and there seemed to be genuine horror in his eye. "Yesterday was something to be shared by only you and me, Marie. As I told you already, I would never tell another soul of it. You need to learn to trust me."

He was right.

"Then how did they know?"

He raised his hands. "When my mother spoke to me of it, she thought that you had been with Lord Downe."

Marie gasped.

"Lord Downe! Why ever would she think that? You didn't believe her?"

"Of course I didn't," he said with a sigh. "I'm sorry, Marie, I didn't mean to make everything worse."

"I know," she said softly, looking down at her hands. "Why don't we talk about this later? The guests will begin to wonder where we've gone off to."

"Does it really matter what they think?"

"Yes," she said, eyeing him with a pointed stare. "It does — to me, at least. Meet me in the library tonight at half past four and we will discuss this further."

"Very well," he said with a slight bow. "Until then."

13

Marie sat nervously on the settee, eyeing the library door. Where was he? He must be at least ten minutes late by now. Was the man never on time? She assumed not. Did he not realize that others were waiting on him? She rolled her eyes as she stood up and began to pace, before finally walking over to a row of bookshelves to try to find something while she waited. Surely, he must be coming soon. And when he did ... what was she going to say? That she didn't want to live with his mother? That she was worried he would take a mistress? He would simply laugh, brush it off, say what she wanted to hear, and then with his delicious looks and charm, he would make her forget she even had any questions.

For that, she could only be upset with herself.

She jumped when the door opened and quickly closed, and she peeked out from behind the bookshelf. "Lionel?" she called when the room offered no one within its depths. She nearly called out again when she heard a sudden noise behind her. "Lio—" but her words were lost when someone's palm suddenly covered her mouth as an arm came around her waist and pulled her back into the shelves' recesses.

"Hello, darling," came a voice in her ear, a voice that sent shivers running down her spine.

Oh, God, help me. Lord Downe.

"How lovely of you to be waiting for me at such a late hour."

He let go of her briefly, but as she tried to run, he only caught her again and turned her around to face him. She opened her mouth to scream for help but he simply laughed. "Do you honestly think you will be heard? The library is far from the bedchambers and no one else is about. The servants are abed as are all of the guests. You timed your little tryst at a most convenient time, I must say."

"You are correct, Lord Downe," she said, maintaining her calm exterior. "Lionel will be here any moment. And then what?"

"Ah, but that is where you are wrong, my Marie." As he smiled, his out-of-fashion beard quivered, and she was utterly repulsed by the dangerous gleam in his eyes. "You told my sister of this assignation, and she told *me* out of concern for you, knowing what she did about the duke. I had her send the duke a message, rearranging the time for you. He will be here, it is true, though he is set to arrive at a most inopportune moment, I assure you. And since you are to appear to be my lover, I thought why do we not make it the truth?"

"You are disgusting," Marie bit out, before protesting, "And Jane would never do such a thing, to follow along with your sinister plans."

"She was worried for you, with all she knew regarding

the duke," he said with a shrug. "Besides, blood will always be more important to her than friendship. You must realize that, Marie."

"Do *not* try to ruin my friendship with Jane. What do you want with me?" she bit out, knowing what he was after and yet wanting to force him to say the words aloud.

He took a step toward her, trying to close the little space that remained between them. She jumped back but hit the bookshelf behind her, and he laughed, his teeth the only thing she could see very well in the slice of moonlight that streamed in through the windows.

"Well, darling, all I am supposed to do is to make it seem as though we are having a liaison. It shouldn't be incredibly difficult, for you already know what that is all about, do you not?"

"It was you!" she said, fury edging out some of the desperate panic that filled her. "*You* spread the lie to Lady Catherine. But why would you even think I had done such a thing?"

"I saw your lover exit your room that afternoon, fixing his cravat as he went," Lord Downe sneered. "Giving yourself away like a common whore. Tsk, tsk, Marie, you were raised better than that! The dowager duchess wants nothing to do with your family, as I was aware after overhearing a conversation. Fortunately for you, I will still have you despite the mar you now carry upon your name. I had thought if I could convince the dowager duchess that you and I were together, it would be enough. But sadly your duke did not believe the tale so now I must make it true."

"You wouldn't *dare*," Marie bit out, incredulous that he would even think to do such a thing. What in heaven's name was wrong with the man? And Lionel's mother ... she had known the woman hated her, it was true, but this was incredible.

"Oh I *would* dare," he said with relish. "Now come here, Marie, let me taste you."

As he leaned in, she brought her hands to his arms as though she were welcoming his embrace. Far from it, however, as she used his own appendages as leverage to bring her knee up and into his groin. He gave a shout and dropped his arms to hold himself in pain, and Marie took the opportunity to dart out of his grasp and bolt for the exit. She had always been quick, her step sure, and she would have made it had he not locked the library doors. She pulled on the handle, but it wouldn't budge. She fumbled in her pocket for the key, but it kept slipping out of her grasp as her fingers were trembling with nerves. She let out a sob of relief when she found the right key, and after a few attempts, she fit it into the keyhole. When she turned it, the click was the most heavenly sound in the entire world. She put her hand to the brass knob, but just when she was about to pull, Lord Downe grabbed her from behind.

"No!" she shouted, tears beginning to fall down her face as she looked desperately around her for a way out of this. She fought him, bringing a heel down on his toe, but her kid slippers did nothing to him through the leather of his boot. She dug her nails into his hand, kicked backward with her heel, but it was of no use. He tossed her on the settee but before she could roll off, he was there, atop of her, his breath reeking of cheroots and sour wine.

"Don't fight it, darling," he said, his head coming down toward her, his hand inching up her bodice.

"Don't call me that!" she yelled, bringing her hand up and driving the heel of it into his nose.

"Ouch!" he yelped but didn't move, his weight holding her down. "You've bloodied my nose!"

"Good," she seethed as she squirmed to try to find a way out of this, to escape him. It was then that the door slammed open. As Lord Downe's head turned to the entrance, she brought her hand back and directed her fist at his face once more, giving a cry when it connected with his cheekbone.

She heard a roar from the entrance, and in stormed Lionel. She shouted his name as tears of relief now rained down her face. Marie gasped when he lifted Lord Downe off of her as though he were a doll, flinging him over the square ottoman and onto the floor. Lionel scooped her up into his arms as though she weighed nothing before stalking out, kicking the door behind him.

"Are you all right, love?" he asked gently, though she could see fury swimming beneath the surface of his eyes.

"Yes," she said breathily as she tried to compose herself, despite the hiccups she heard that must be coming from her, for who else would be hiccuping in the upper corridor of Hollyvalle? "Th-thank you, Lionel. He was going to— he was going to—"

"I know," he said before gathering her close, rocking her back and forth as though she were a little child. "I know."

LIONEL HAD NEVER BEEN SO furious in his entire life. A beast had taken over him as he had stormed into the library and seen Downe sitting atop Marie. He had lost all thought, acting purely on primal instinct as he picked him up and threw him. He had wanted nothing more but to follow him over to where he lay on the library floor and continue the beating Marie had begun with her plucky little fists, but first he had to see to his lady.

He held her close now, continuing to reassure himself that she was all right.

"Do you have the key, love?"

"It's on the other side," she said, her voice raspy, and he opened the door just wide enough to find the key before slamming it again and locking it from the outside. "There," he said. "That should hold him until I return."

He continued down the hallway, carrying her up the stairs and along the corridor to her own bedroom. He lay her down gently before running his eyes as well as his hands over her neck, shoulders, and arms, trying to reassure himself she wasn't injured. The only mark on her was her bruised knuckle. He wet a cloth from the washbasin in the corner and covered her knuckles with it.

"He didn't ... do anything to you?" he asked again, and relief flooded through him when she shook her head.

"No, Lionel, you came just in time," she said softly. "How did you know to come when you did?"

"My mother's maid," he said, his hands coming to his hips. "She heard the entire sordid plan the two of them put together, and she came to find me. Said she couldn't have it on her conscience. I am disgusted and horrified and so ashamed of my family, Marie. Will you forgive me?"

"It is not your fault, not at all," she said, her eyes wide as she sat up in bed, her dark hair askew, in wild waves about her head.

"I'd best go deal with the man," he said grimly, already trying to determine how he would keep himself from killing him, for every time he thought of what Downe had planned to do, Lionel's blood began to pump furiously with a need to protect what was his.

"Lionel, would you...." Marie chewed her lip. "Would you mind staying with me for a moment instead? I don't feel like being alone."

"Of course," he said, abandoning all that was pressing to be there for Marie. Downe could wait. His love was more important.

14

Marie snuggled deeper into Lionel's warm embrace. Why was he always so fiery? He was the heat to her ice, she supposed, and she closed her eyes and sighed.

"Lionel?"

"Yes?"

"I'm sorry I ever doubted you. I was being proud and vain and allowing the thoughts and concerns of others to come before what I knew to be true. I should have—"

"I understand," he interrupted her in his low, throaty timbre. "My past did not give you much reason to believe in me."

"Oh, I should have still—"

"Hush," he said, turning her over to face him, and he brought a finger to her lips. "It doesn't mean anything now. All that matters is that the two of us have truly found one another. You continued to question whether I care, Marie, and let me tell you this. It is true there is little that concerns me. I figure there is so much with which one could worry over in life, why not just allow things to happen as they will and enjoy the moment? That doesn't, however, mean that I do not have a place in my heart for what is truly important. And nothing means more to me than you, Marie. I don't care for you, no, that is not the right word for it. I love you, with all of my heart and soul. When I thought, for a moment, that something could have happened to you, I nearly lost my mind — and my heart. Marry me, Marie, not just because our fathers deemed it to be, but because you want it so."

Tears burned her eyes and began leaking down her face at his words. Her eyes searched his, at the tender warmth that burned within their blue depths, and as his burly arms came around her, she began to sob in earnest.

"What's this?" he asked, his look of love turning into one of despair. "Do you not ... do you not feel the same?"

"Oh, of course I feel the same!" she said as she wiped her eyes. "I love you more than I could ever have imagined and I want nothing more than to be your wife, whenever you will have me."

A wide grin broke out onto his face.

"Ah love, you had me worried for a moment there."

Somehow a giggle came out through her tears, and she burrowed in even closer to him. He passed her a handkerchief, and she used it to attempt to return some semblance of order to her face.

"You, worried?" she asked after she had composed herself.

"Only by you," he said, and his face descended, his lips capturing hers in a soft, sweet kiss. She clung to him, her arms wrapping around his neck and pulling him close. His kiss was cleansing, washing away the filth left by Lord Downe.

Lionel's touch encased her like a purifying light, causing

her to feel as though she would always be safe with him nearby. She vowed to be the woman he needed in his life, to fill any void required.

When his arms came about her, his fingertips stroking light circles around her back, she sighed into his mouth, closing her eyes and losing herself in him.

Her hands came up into his hair, and she rolled over top of him, her arms encasing his face like a tiny frame around a sculpture.

"Are you sure you want this now, love, after everything that happened?" he asked, his voice a husky whisper.

"I don't want it," she said, her eyes searching his face, memorizing every detail. "I need it."

Her lips descended, their kiss no longer soft but unyielding now, as she accepted from him all the joy and freedom he offered her. His strong hands caressed her back, unlacing the silky thread of her dress as he did. She found the buttons of his shirt, and, slightly more practiced now, she began undoing them without breaking her lips from his. When he groaned deeply into her mouth, she felt a sense of power rise within her, and for the first time, she became aware of just how wonderful it was to know such influence over a man — especially this man.

She pulled the linen shirt over his head, taking a moment to sit back and admire the bulge of his muscle beneath. He was nothing like the slim, slight men she knew. He reminded her of a warrior from the days of old.

Marie slowly removed one arm from her dress, followed by the other, keeping her eyes locked on his the entire time. She saw the desperation there as he watched her movements, and she smiled wickedly at him. When the material pooled around her waist, he finally broke his stillness, sitting up and lifting her to free her of the dress, before helping to divest her of her stays and chemise.

His big hands encircled her waist as he held her straddled above him.

"Oh, Marie," he groaned. "I cannot take much more of this."

She brought a finger to his lips to silence him before she trailed her fingers over his chin, his neck, and his chest, his body straining at her slight touch. She continued down his abdomen, finding the silky trail of hair that led lower.

"No," he said, his voice hoarse. "You ... you..."

"I said shh," she continued, looking up at him crossly before she brought her mouth to him, testing, tasting, to see how he reacted.

And react he did. He gave a shout, just managing to control the volume of his cry so he didn't wake the entire household. Liking the control, she took more of him in her mouth, but it didn't last long as he apparently could no longer stand it, and he lifted her up before bringing her down slowly on top of him.

She gasped as he easily slid into her, and she began to move instinctually, though she felt her movements were somewhat lacking precision. He helped her, using his hands to move her hips back and forth, and before long she caught on and he let go, giving her complete control. The beginnings of that feeling she had experienced before began anew, and she didn't know whether the heat engulfing her was coming from him or was of her own doing. Just when she didn't think she could take any more of the indescribable feeling flowing through her veins, it exploded within her, and as she threw her head back, she heard Lionel let out a cry himself as he found his own release.

Marie fell down against his chest, and for a moment, she

couldn't move as she reveled in the after effects. All she could do was smile at the fact that she could have this — have *him* — for the rest of her life.

MARIE OPENED HER EYES LAZILY, as something pervaded the wonderful dream she was having, and she willed it to go away so she could go back to the fantasy she was having about Lionel.

"Go away," she mumbled, and then she heard the tap again on the door.

"My lady?" Lydia. What time was it? And why was she so tired? She threw a hand over her head and rolled over — right into a hard, warm body.

"Ah!" she gave a bit of a cry as the memories — the upsetting and the wonderful — from last night came flooding back. So they weren't a dream after all.

"My lady, are you awake? There is an awful row going on. It seems Lord Downe was found locked in the library and he has all sort of accusations regarding you and ... and..."

"And me," came the deep voice beside her, and Marie swatted him and told him to hush, but he only grinned at her.

"One moment, Lydia," she called out, and Lionel began to button his shirt. He stood once he was nearly dressed, and Marie looked wildly around to determine how to hide him, but Lionel waved his hand in the air.

"Let her in," he said. "We'll be married soon anyway, and there will be worse scandal once we go downstairs and confront Lord Downe."

"But — oh, very well," she said, no longer wanting to put up a fight. "Come in, Lydia."

"My lady— oh!" Lydia said, shock on her face as she looked from Marie to Lionel and back again.

"Lydia," Marie said, sitting tall in the bed despite the fact she wore only her undergarments. "You have been with me for some time now, and I hope that it will remain that way. I am trusting that you will tell no one of what you have seen here. The duke and I will soon be married, so this is a sight you may see from time to time."

"Y-yes, my lady," she said, and after a moment of hesitation, she rushed to the wardrobe. "But you had best get dressed right away. Your parents require your presence immediately."

"Very well," Marie said with a sigh, and then she turned to Lionel. "You'd best get going now," she said with a smile. "I will see you shortly."

He nodded, winked, and then was out the door.

LIONEL SAT across from Lord Downe, wishing he could jump across the library and pummel the man into the floor with his fists. But the time for that had passed and they were now sitting with Marie's family, the other guests kept unaware for the moment, though Lionel knew this sort of thing always made its way around from one ear to the next. He slouched low in his chair as he took in the man sitting across from him.

He and Marie each recounted their stories, the Marquess of St. James' face growing angrier by the moment, until it was splotched a mottled red.

The marquess rose and made his way over to Lord

Downe, who tried to protest that it was not as they had said, but that it was *he* had discovered *them*.

"Get out of my house," the marquess ground out. "And never, ever return. I shall make sure all the peerage is made aware of what has happened here, and *you*, Downe, will be lucky to find any sort of respectable woman who will want you. Now go!"

His last words came out as a roar, and the man practically ran for the door. He shot a dark look at Lionel on his way out, but Lionel simply grinned.

"Well," the marquess said in a huff, pacing the room, his anger apparently not quite sated. "Well."

"Lord St. James," Lionel said, sitting up in his chair now, smoothing back his hair. "I meant what I said earlier. I should like to marry Marie as soon as possible, and I believe — I hope — that she feels the same."

"I do, Father," she said, from where she sat on the settee beside her mother, her hands clasped in her lap.

"Oh?" the marquess said, his eyebrows raised. "And what has brought on such a change?"

"Simply that I have gotten to know Lio— the duke," she said, casting a small smile his way. "And I have realized that I would be lucky to have him as a husband after all."

"Very good," the marquess said, puffing out his chest. "I shall make sure all is in order."

And with that, he marched out the door, apparently to his office. Marie's mother looked from her daughter to Lionel with a small, knowing smile, before following her husband out the door.

Lionel quickly strode across the room, taking Marie's hands in his as he knelt before her.

"How are you?" he asked softly, wondering how the entire ordeal had affected her.

She looked up at him, and he noted how her eyes were the blue of an aquamarine gemstone. He would have to buy one for her after their wedding, he decided, but his thoughts were interrupted with her words.

"Lionel," she said slowly. "I do not think I shall ever understand the lackadaisical way you approach life. But I have realized that I do not have to — I simply need to be aware that you will be there when something truly matters, and despite what you show others on the surface, you do care about many things — and people — even if you do not show it. And perhaps I need a bit more freeness of spirit in my life."

"Perhaps you do," he said, his lips twitching, though he could tell she wouldn't welcome laughter at this moment. "I always thought, Marie, that taking a wife would mean additional responsibility that I was not prepared for. Now I have the feeling that you will actually take much responsibility away from me. For you seem to be a woman who would enjoy running a household."

"Every bit of it," she said with flourish. "I was born for it. But...."

"My mother."

"Yes, your mother."

"There is a fine dowager house on my property. My mother will have to be content with moving her possessions there and not entering our home. I cannot throw her out on the street, but she will have no contact with you, Marie. If she does bother you, then I will purchase a home for her in London, and she can move there. I always knew she was the vengeful sort, but her actions have been inexcusable."

Marie nodded, solemn at the thought of the lengths to which the woman was willing to go in order to get what she wanted, and sad for the loss of the relationship between mother and son, though Lionel had assured her there hadn't been much of one.

"And our wedding, Lionel, it can be how I choose?"

"As long as it's soon, Marie, it can be however you choose."

"Very well," she said, a grin stretching over her face. He had no idea what he had just agreed to.

EPILOGUE

Twenty-six years later

Marie looked around the table at her children. She loved them equally, of course, and she worried about them all with equal measure. She was pleased that they had all come home for Christmas dinner, though she wished at least one of them had a family to speak of.

"Daniel," she said, trying to reach her eldest son, who had become so withdrawn from the family after the death of the woman he was courting that it physically hurt her. "How fares your estate, darling? I know you are so committed to it."

"Fine, Mother," he said, his gaze returning to the goose on his plate.

She sighed and looked around at the rest of them. They were laughing, jovial, from her eldest daughter Violet, who she knew was so like herself and ready to find love, to her second eldest son, Thomas. He looked over at her with a smile, and she returned it, though she was concerned for him. He was trying to find his way in the world, which was never easy for a second son. He had a commission in the navy, and she was worried that he had the wrong expectations of what that would provide him. She supposed he could only determine that for himself.

"Something wrong, Mother?" Benjamin asked with a wink at her, and she shook her head at her mischievous youngest son. The exact opposite of Daniel, he was always looking for the next bit of a fun in his life — far too like his father had been in his youth, though Lionel was determined Benjamin never find out about that.

"Not at all," she said, and her youngest, the beautiful Polly with the blond hair of Marie's father, took her hand gave it a squeeze. "Relax, Mother," she said. "It's Christmas."

"So it is, darling," she said and turned to look at her husband. He winked at her, and while his face was thicker and a few more lines creased the corner of his eyes and mouth, it was the same wink that had charmed her all of those years ago.

Five children later, he still knew the right words to say to her to calm her down — or excite her, if the case might be. They had found a rhythm to their life, to their pairing. Whatever he could care less about, she perhaps cared too much. And if she became too involved in something, well, he was always there to thoughtfully tell her that perhaps she needed to step away. Not that she ever took that with much grace, but at times, it needed to be said.

The Yule log crackled in the fireplace. Marie loved Christmas, especially once they had welcomed children, and she insisted on one log for each of them throughout the home. The dining room seemed fitting, as it was where they had always gathered. She knew her children were a bit too loud, a bit too boisterous, but Lionel liked it that way, and she had to admit that in this, she had come around to his way of thinking.

The dinner passed all too quickly, and before long the night was over and Marie found herself upstairs, alone with her husband.

"Marie," he said as he hoisted himself into bed and patted the place beside him. "Come here, darling."

She turned from where she was brushing her hair. "Now?"

"Yes, now. Please."

"Very well," she said with a shrug, placing her hairbrush back on the vanity. Lionel didn't often ask for much, so she had learned to listen when he did.

He reached into a drawer beside him and brought out a small package. "I have something for you. A gift for Christmas."

"Oh?" she asked, raising an eyebrow. "I thought we exchanged gifts already."

"I know," he said as he looked down at the package. "But this is something ... special."

She took the long paper-wrapped package from him, tearing it away to reveal its contents, gasping when she did. For their inside was a painting, depicting a couple skating over a frozen pond on a clear winter's day.

"Oh Lionel," she said with a tear in her eye. "This is exquisite. And the pair — why, they look just like we did that very day we skated."

"They are," he said with a smile. "I had it painted for you. For I'll never forget that day — the day I fell in love with you. Because of you, Marie, Christmas will always be the day when my new life began. You brought love to my life, family to my heart, and I can never thank you enough. I love you, Marie, and I always will."

"And I love you, Lionel," she said, her heart full near to bursting. "Happy Christmas, my love."

THE END

~

Sign-up for Ellie's email list and "Unmasking a Duke," a regency romance, will come straight to your inbox — free!

www.prairielilypress.com/ellies-newsletter/

You will also receive links to giveaways, sales, updates, launch information, promos, and the newest recommended reads.

QUEST OF HONOR

SEARCHING HEARTS BOOK 1

PREVIEW

Begin the stories of the Harrington's children with Thomas and Eleanor...

PROLOGUE

Marie looked around the table at her five children, her gaze coming to rest on Thomas. Normally she was most concerned about Daniel, her eldest and the next in line to become Duke, but there was something about Thomas tonight that seemed off to her.

Typically the most free-spirited of her children, this evening he wore a serious look, and had taken on the brooding silence that overcame him whenever he felt stifled or frustrated.

The remainder of her children, from Daniel at 24 down to her 16-year-old daughter Polly, were chattering away as they were normally wont to do, no matter how she tried to instil in them the proper etiquette of the dinner hour. Her husband, Lionel, Duke of Ware, sat in his usual place at the head of the table, intent on his food as he listened to the stories of his brood.

"Thomas," Marie said, and he raised his dark head. "Is everything quite well, darling?"

"Yes, Mother," he replied mechanically.

"Are you quite sure?"

"Well actually," he said, looking hesitantly at her and then his father. "I do have somewhat of an announcement."

Marie raised her eyebrows as the chatter around the table hushed, for Thomas' siblings could see the nervousness that accompanied his statement.

"I am going to be joining the Navy," he said, puffing his chest out, trying to look more assured than he felt.

"The Navy!" his mother exclaimed incredulously. "You cannot be serious. Is this some sort of joke?"

"Not at all, Mother," he responded, his blue eyes taking on an icy resolve. "The Navy is a noble profession. What else am I to do with my life?"

"You are the second son of a Duke! What if the title of Duke should need to pass onto you and you are injured or dead somewhere at sea?"

"I shall not spend my life sitting here waiting for Father and Daniel to die, Mother," he responded, his voice becoming slightly more heated, although he would never raise it at his mother. "They are both quite healthy and, I'm sure, have long lives to live. I want to see the world! What better way than on the sea?"

"Lionel!" Marie said to her husband with fervour. "Have you nothing to say?"

Lionel finished chewing his potatoes, his expression unwavering.

"Well, son," he said. "I would say your intentions are admirable. You do know what you are getting yourself into?"

"I do."

"Well, then, boy, I'd best talk to my friend the Admiral tomorrow. The son of the Duke of Ware must find a reasonable berth and vessel upon which to serve."

Thomas' face lit up, and he caught the gaze of his sister

Violet, who smiled at him encouragingly. He grinned at her, then turned back to his father.

"Thank you, Father," he said. "I would appreciate it."

"This is quite ridiculous," his mother said, her head swivelling from Thomas to Lionel and back to Thomas once more. "Thomas is 22 years old! He and Daniel should be finding wives, settling down, raising children. Instead, Daniel is out doing Heaven knows what and Thomas will be at sea miles away from Britain! How is it that I have three children of marriageable age, none of which have any interest in actually being married?"

Benjamin and Polly smirked, happy to have the attention off of them and onto their three elder siblings.

"In due time, Mother," said Violet, somewhat mollifying her. "In due time. In the meantime, let us drink to Thomas and the world that awaits him."

"To Thomas!" They all joined in, with the exception of Marie, and Thomas grinned, excited about what the future would hold for him.

1

Five years later

Eleanor Adams sat primly on the straight backed chair as her father stomped around, muttering something under his breath. She waited patiently for his judgement to fall, knowing that he would not be able to bring himself to punish her too severely. After all, she was his only child and he had never been able to be too strict with her. In fact, this was the only life Eleanor had ever known. Just her and her father, facing the world and all its tribulations.

"You cannot simply do as you please, Eleanor!" her father spluttered, his face now a beetroot red. "What if we had not seen you?"

Eleanor stifled a sigh of frustration. "Papa, you know me better than that. I simply *had* to investigate whatever it was down there." A small smile crept across her face. "And, if I had not, then we would currently not have these three small trunks in our possession." She indicated the three, still damp, trunks that sat beside her father's desk, glancing at them before returning her gaze to her father.

To her very great relief, he sighed and sat down heavily, although he continued to shake his head at her. Eleanor hid her smile. She was triumphant.

"We have not opened them yet, Eleanor," her father said, a little gruffly. "You could have risked your life for nothing."

In response, Eleanor tossed her head, aware of the spots of moisture that shook off her long flaxen locks. "I am one of the best swimmers among the crew, Papa, you know that."

"But still," he retorted. "You cannot just dive off the ship without alerting someone to what you have found! Had you done so, I could have dropped the anchor and gone to see what was there."

Eleanor bit her lip, aware that her father was being more than reasonable. Had any one of his crew done what she had, they would have been severely punished. It was only because she was the captain's daughter that she had done such a thing. Her cheeks warmed. "I was trying to prove myself, Papa," she explained, more quietly. "As the only woman on board, I have to take extra steps to show my worth."

His face softened. "Eleanor, you already have my respect and the respect of the crew. For over twenty years you have traveled the seas with us and you have no need to prove yourself. Doing such a thing is both dangerous and shows a lack of regard for me – not only as your father but also as your captain." His lined face grew more serious, as his bushy eyebrows clung together. "You know that I will need to punish you for what you did, Eleanor. As much as it pains me to do this, you are to be confined to your quarters for two days."

"Two days?" Eleanor gasped, staring at her father. "But I will miss the exploration!"

Her father nodded gravely. "I have to show the crew that I am not afraid to punish you, even though you are my daughter." A hint of a smile pulled up the corner of his lips. "Just be glad it is not the cat o'nine tails, Eleanor."

Eleanor sagged against the chair, her ladylike position gone in a moment. Reflecting on her father's decision, she had to admit that it was fair, lenient even. She hated that her impulsive nature had, once again, brought severe consequences. If only she had not dived into the water to see what it was that glistened below! If she had only told her father, then he would have dropped the anchor and sent someone down – although Eleanor doubted that he would have chosen her. Even though she could swim like a fish, her father always kept her in his sights whenever he could.

"I am sorry you will miss the exploration of the Blackmoor Caves," her father continued, gently. "But Eleanor, you must know that you cannot simply do what you please on this ship."

"I do know, Papa," Eleanor replied, dully, ashamed that her the whole ordeal caused her to feel like a child when she would prefer to be treated as the sailor she was. She could only hope the treasure would yield results that would make all forget about the find and focus on the outcome. "I'm sorry."

Her father placed a gentle hand on her shoulder, getting to his feet. "Like you say, however, we have retrieved three trunks."

Hope sparked in Eleanor's chest. "You mean, I can open them?"

He chuckled. "I think so. After all, you were the one who spotted the locks gleaming under the ocean's waves."

Eleanor rose, her booted feet clattering across the wooden floor of the cabin as she made her way towards the trunks. She would have to change into dry clothing, but that could wait. "It is only because we are in such shallow waters," she said, bending down to examine the trunks. "Had the water been any deeper, then I doubt we would have found them."

"Here." Her father handed her a large mallet, and, using all her strength, Eleanor hit the lock.

It broke easily, evidently having been underwater for some time. With bated breath, Eleanor pushed the top of the trunk back. A wide grin spread across her face as she took in the bounty.

"There is some gold here," she cried, pulling out a gold coin and handing it to her father. "Not much, but enough."

Chuckling, her father picked up the mallet and broke the other two locks, finding more gold and some silver in the other two trunks. He crowed with delight as he grasped great handfuls of coins, letting them trickle back down into the trunk. Despite her impending punishment, Eleanor could not help but smile too, delighted that they would have more than enough to pay the crew for the next quarter.

"Everyone shall have a bonus!" her father declared, getting to his feet and throwing open the door to his cabin. "Morgan!"

The first mate came stumbling in, as though he'd been waiting for the captain to call his name. "Aye, Captain Adams?"

Eleanor grinned as her father slapped Morgan on the back, before gesturing towards the treasure.

"Here," he said. "Sort this out. Crew's pay and a bonus for everyone. Leave the remaining treasure in the first trunk."

Morgan returned Eleanor's smile, and got to the task at once, jubilant over some of the wonders he was finding. It would take him an age to sort out the treasure into piles of equal worth, but Eleanor knew it was a job the first mate thoroughly enjoyed.

Wiping down her breeches, Eleanor got to her feet and smiled at her father, wondering if he might forget her punishment.

Unfortunately, he had not.

"Right, Eleanor, to your cabin. Your meals will be sent down."

A sigh left her lips as she trudged past him, sniffing inelegantly. Behind her, she heard her father chuckle.

"Two days will be over before you know it, my dear," he said, following her out. "And if we find anything at the caves, you may join in the salvaging."

That was a slight relief, making her shoulders rise from their slumped position. "Thank you, Papa," she mumbled, as the fresh air hit her lungs. Taking in another few breaths, Eleanor took in the smell of the sea, the wind whipping at her hair....before she realized that the entire crew was watching her.

Taking a breath, she lifted her chin. "I should not have dived off the boat without alerting someone to what I had found," she said, loudly. "I did you all wrong by acting so impulsively and showed disrespect to our captain. I will not do such a thing again." She caught the look of sympathy in some of the crew's eyes, although they appeared to be relieved that she was receiving some kind of punishment. Without another word, Eleanor turned on her heel and walked down the short staircase to her cabin below.

Being the only woman meant she had one of only two tiny cabins below deck – Morgan, the first mate, held the other. Pulling open the door, she looked glumly into her gloomy room, hating that she would be stuck inside for two days.

"Thank you for your apology, Eleanor," her father said, holding the door as she walked inside. "The crew respects you, as they do me. They will hold you in greater esteem because you have confessed your wrongs."

Eleanor tried to smile, sitting down heavily on the wooden bed. "Thank you, Papa. I believe the treasure I found for them may also have increased their sense of 'esteem' in me."

He grinned at her. "You're a pirate's daughter, Eleanor. Some might think that means we have no standards, no way of keeping control, but you know how precarious the sea – and the crew – can be. They are loyal to me, and I want them to be loyal to you too. One day, this boat might be yours." With a quick smile, he closed the door and left her to her thoughts.

Eleanor stared at the door, her father's words echoing around her mind. One day, she might have control of the ship? Be the captain? Could such a thing truly happen?

Eleanor knew that in the Navy, there would be no thought of having a female captain, but they were far removed from the Navy! Pirates did things differently and, if her father thought the crew would respect her as captain, then she would gladly step into the role, though she hoped it would be some time before her father gave it up and retired from the seas.

To be a pirate captain! The thought made her smile, despite her current situation. To roam the seas with her crew, searching for bounty and, in their case, helping those less fortunate. She could not think of a better life.

QUEST OF HONOR *is now available for purchase on Amazon and to read free in Kindle Unlimited!*

THE DUKE SHE WISHED FOR

HAPPILY EVER AFTER BOOK 1

PREVIEW
Go back to the beginning and read the story of Tabitha and
Nicholas...

CHAPTER 1

The creak of the shop's front door opening floated through the heavy curtains that separated Tabitha's workshop from the sales floor. She tensed over the silk ribbon she was attempting to fashion into a flower shape and waited for the sound of her stepsister Frances to greet whoever had just walked into the Blackmore Milliner shop.

She paused, waiting a little bit longer before pushing out a frustrated breath and standing. These velvet ribbon flowers she had learned to fashion were part of the reason Blackmore hats sat atop some of the finest female heads in polite society — she had a knack for creating new ways to adorn the same old bonnet or beaver hat styles so that a woman of a certain class stood out among her peers.

This ability was both a blessing and a curse, it turned out. Her creativity meant Tabitha brought customers through the front door, to the shop she and her father had built after her mother died when she was seven years old. It had brought Tabitha and her father, the baronet Elias Blackmore, closer together in their time of immeasurable grief, and the shop had flourished.

The relationship between father and daughter remained strong, and when she was twelve years of age, he approached her and told her he wanted to marry a baroness from the North Country. The baroness had a daughter about her own age, he'd added. Tabitha had been happy for her father and excited at the prospect of having a sister. She had welcomed her new family with an open heart and open arms.

What a silly little fool she'd been, Tabitha thought with derisive snort as she pushed herself to her feet and through the brocade curtains to greet the newcomer. Lord only knew where Frances had gone off to. Likely shopping with her mother, Ellora.

Upon the untimely death of Sir Elias Blackmore three years after the marriage, Tabitha had been utterly devastated. Lady Blackmore, however, hadn't wasted much time in putting Tabitha in her place. No longer the family's most cherished daughter, Tabitha had been shoved into the workroom and largely ignored, but for her skills as a milliner — they kept just enough of her stepmother's attention on her.

The more she stood up to Ellora, the more her stepmother threatened to throw her out on the street. Knowing it was within Ellora's nature to follow through on her threat, Tabitha did her best to ignore and avoid her stepmother, focusing instead on her work and her ambitions.

It was better, Tabitha supposed, than staying in their townhome all day long worrying about social calls that never came or invitations that would never arrive. The family name had suffered greatly under Lady Blackmore and Miss Frances Denner, her daughter from a previous marriage.

In truth, Tabitha was little more than a servant with no money to speak of, no family to lean on, and no real prospects other than her creations on which to pin her hopes of ever escaping the lot she'd been given after her father died.

In the showroom, Tabitha scanned the floor in search of the new arrival. It took a moment, but her eyes finally landed on a small, older man in a fine suit. He had a slip of paper in his hand, and he approached Tabitha with the air of someone who didn't waste time.

"Good afternoon, Miss," the man began with perfect, practiced speech. "My name is Mr. McEwan. I serve as the steward in the house of Her Grace the Duchess of Stowe. I have a receipt for a series of hats I believe she had ordered, and she is requesting that they be delivered tomorrow afternoon."

Tabitha felt her stomach sink. If this was the order she was thinking of, the one currently on her worktable, there was no way under the stars that the three hats would be ready by tomorrow. She was only one flower (out of seven) into the first bonnet, and it was a slow process to convince the requested velvet ribbon to behave.

"I am sorry, sir," she began, trying to get his eyes off the wilder ostrich-plumed hats next to her and back on her. "That is almost four days before we agreed upon. I'm certain there is no feasible way the work can be done, and done well, by tomorrow."

That got the older man's attention. He huffed, turned a bit pink around the cheeks, and sputtered.

"There is simply no choice, my dear," he said abruptly but not unkindly. "His Grace is arriving home from his trip to France early and therefore the parties his mother has planned for him will be adjusted accordingly. And so, her wardrobe *must* be ready — she said so herself. She is willing to pay handsomely for your ability to expedite the process."

Tabitha drew in a breath at that and considered. She was having such a difficult time scrimping a small savings together to buy herself a seat at the Paris School of Millinery that this "bonus" money might perhaps get her there that much quicker. Assuming, of course, that Ellora didn't catch wind of the extra earnings. She was quick to snatch up all but the barest pennies.

Tabitha closed her eyes for a moment and drew a steadying breath. If she worked through the night and her needle and thread held true, there was a *slight* chance that she could finish in time. She said so to Mr. McEwan, who beamed brightly at her.

"I knew it," he said with a laugh. "I have faith you Miss — er, I apologize, I did not hear your name?"

Tabitha sighed.

"Tabitha Blackmore," she said, noticing how quickly he'd changed the subject on her. "I did not exactly say that I would be able to—"

She was cut off again by Mr. McEwan, who gave her a slight bow and provided directions to the home of the Dowager Duchess of Stowe on the other side of the city.

"I shall see you tomorrow, then, my dear," he said with a quick grin. "Be sure to pack a bag to stay at least one evening, maybe two. I am certain Her Grace's attendants will need proper coaching on how best to pair the hats. You will be paid, of course!"

With that the short man with wisps of white hair on his head that stood up like smoke was gone, disappearing into the streets of Cheapside.

Tabitha leaned back against the counter behind her and blew out a breath, a little overwhelmed at the entire encounter.

On the one hand, she had found a way to increase her

savings and take a step closer to the education her father had wanted for her. On the other, getting through the night in one piece was not guaranteed. She would have to return to the shop after dinner and do so without rousing Lady Blackmore's suspicions, which would not be easy.

Tabitha kicked at a crushed crepe ribbon flower that hadn't been tossed out properly. Another evening down the back drainpipe it was, then.

"Time away from the witch, I suppose," she muttered as she returned to her worktable, a new fire of inspiration lit beneath her.

Dinner was more complicated than usual, thanks to the fact that Ellora, Tabitha's stepmother, was having one of her *moods*. They could be brought on by anything — the weather (too foul or too pleasant), the noisy street they lived on, memories of her life when she was the daughter of an earl and had endless opportunities for money and titles, or even an egg that had too much salt.

Today's mood, however, had more to do with the fact that her daughter Frances had been recently snubbed. Officially, Ellora was considered a member of the *ton* and her daughter's first season the previous year had nearly cost them the roof over their heads. However, Frances was an ill-tempered, sharp-tongued girl who did little to ensure repeat invitations to dances and parties.

"A true-and-true witch," their housekeeper, Alice, called her. Alice was the only servant left on staff besides Katie, the lady's maid Ellora and Frances shared, so it was up to both Alice and Tabitha to make sure that meals were made and rooms were kept clean. Being an indentured servant in her own home was trying enough, but much worse was having to tidy the room that once held every memento of her father's. It was now completely devoid of every memory of him.

It was as though Baronet Elias Blackmore had never existed. No portraits. No personal belongings. Nothing but the small locket he'd given Tabitha when she was nine years old, which she still wore around her neck.

This evening's dinner was a morose affair, and Tabitha sat silently while Ellora ranted and raved about the social snub of her angel, Frances.

Tabitha looked across the table at her stepsister. Frances was very pretty, she'd give her that much. But her mouth was drawn thin and her blue eyes were more steely than pleasant. Frances had brown hair that one could call more dishwater in color than brunette. However, Ellora spent high sums of money on beauty products and bits and bobs for Katie to fashion Frances' hair into something resembling high fashion each day.

Frances was pouting into her soup while her mother railed beside her. When she glanced up and caught Tabitha looking at her, she scowled.

Tabitha quickly looked away, but Frances jumped on the opportunity to take the attention off her.

"I saw a servant go into the shop this afternoon when I was returning from tea with Adela," Frances said to her mother, her flinty eyes on Tabitha, who inwardly groaned.

So much for secrecy.

Ellora paused in her ranting and raised an eyebrow at her.

"Who was it?"

The words were clipped, and her nose was high in the air while she peered along it at Tabitha.

"A servant for the Dowager Duchess of Stowe," Tabitha replied. "He came to inquire about an order the Duchess sent over a week ago."

It wasn't exactly a lie and it helped her corroborate her story because Ellora had already received the money sent over for the original order.

"And was the order ready?"

Tabitha swallowed hard. She wasn't in the clear yet.

"Almost," she said and lowered her eyes to take a sip of the soup as she inwardly seethed.

"Unacceptable," her stepmother ground out between her teeth. "You lazy, no-good hanger-on. It is no wonder your father's ridiculous hat shop is dying off. He had the laziest cow this side of the river working behind the curtains."

She banged a fist on the table, making Frances jump.

"You get up from this table and you finish that order right this instant." Ellora pointed a long bony finger in the direction of the door, ending Tabitha's dinner before she had progressed past the soup. Tabitha's stomach rumbled in protest, and her fists clenched beneath the table as she longed to tell Ellora what she really thought, but Tabitha knew this was a gift. She would nab a roll from Alice later.

"I am going to stop by in the morning to check your ledger and work progress to make certain you are being completely honest with me," Ellora announced. "And woe be to you if I find that you have been neglecting your work and you have a backlog of orders."

In reality, Tabitha was of legal age and the threats should be harmless. But she was also lacking any real money, any job prospects, and had no titles her father could have passed down to her. Running her father's milliner shop was the closest thing she would have to freedom for the near future, and it would be much better for her if she allowed Ellora the illusion of control for the time being, since the dreadful woman had inherited the shop upon her father's death.

Ellora's threat put Tabitha in a bind. She was due at the Duchess' estate first thing in the morning. As it stood, she'd have to have those pieces done, as well as the other orders on her workbench before then. She closed her eyes and blew out a heavy breath.

It was going to be a very long night.

The Duke She Wished For is now available for purchase on Amazon, and is free to read through Kindle Unlimited.

ABOUT THE AUTHOR

 Ellie has always loved reading, writing, and history. For many years she has written short stories, non-fiction, and has worked on her true love and passion -- romance novels.

In every era there is the chance for romance, and Ellie enjoys exploring many different time periods, cultures, and geographic locations. No matter when or where, love can always prevail. She has a particular soft spot for the bad boys of history, and loves a strong heroine in her stories.

The lake is Ellie's happy place, and when she's not writing, she is spending time with her son, her Husky/Border Collie cross, and her own dashing duke. She loves reading — of course — as well as running, biking, and summers at the lake.

She also loves corresponding with readers, so be sure to contact her!

www.prairielilypress.com/ellie-st-clair
ellie@prairielilypress.com

facebook.com/elliestclairauthor

twitter.com/ellie_stclair

instagram.com/elliestclairauthor

amazon.com/author/elliestclair

goodreads.com/elliestclair

bookbub.com/authors/elliest.clair

pinterest.com/elliestclair

ALSO BY ELLIE ST. CLAIR

Standalone

Unmasking a Duke

Christmastide with His Countess

Seduced Under the Mistletoe Multi-Author Box Set

(featuring The Duke of Christmas)

Happily Ever After

The Duke She Wished For

Someday Her Duke Will Come

Once Upon a Duke's Dream

He's a Duke, But I Love Him

Loved by the Viscount

Because the Earl Loved Me

Searching Hearts

Quest of Honor

Clue of Affection

Hearts of Trust

Hope of Romance

Promise of Redemption

The Unconventional Ladies

Lady of Mystery

Manufactured by Amazon.ca
Bolton, ON

35454786R00083